About the author

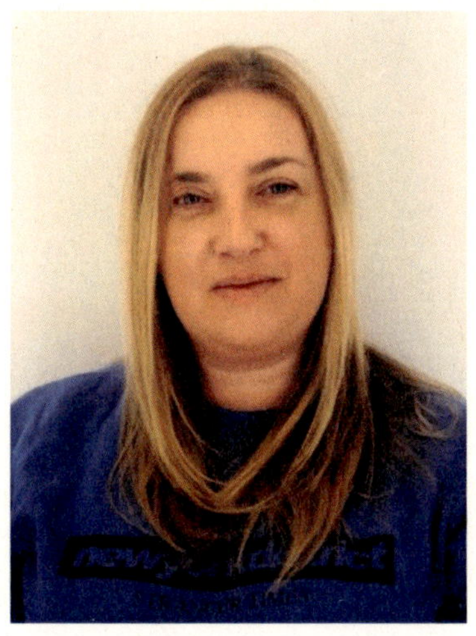

I am a mother of four beautiful children. I was born and raised in Norfolk, growing up in the small town of Diss; but now live in New Zealand. I work full-time as a QA and administrator for a poultry company. I enjoy playing darts and used to play for a local team. I love spending time with my friends and family when I can.

The Boss

Rachael Fisher

The Boss

Chimera

Dedication

I dedicate this book to my children, who are my everything; even if at times I've been far away, you are all fixed in my heart. Also to my best friend, Michelle, who has been by my side for over ten years. She took me and my children in when we had nowhere to go; so for that I am forever grateful.

Death is simply another form of life, but
experienced in a different place.

CHAPTER ONE

Sitting in my old banged-up Ford Escort that I've had since like forever, listening to Celine Dion's 'My Heart Will Go On', I suddenly feel nauseous and dizzy. This is my first day at Hails and Boon venture seed, where their motto is 'You give us the venture and we will plant the seed'. It's down King Street in the busy town of Norwich, and is something I've never done before. What if I walk in and they hate me? What if the place is run by jumped-up twenty-year-olds on power trips? Oh god, I feel sick. I haven't even met my boss – I was interviewed by some middle-aged man from another branch. I mean, how does he know I'll be good for a job that he won't even be working at? I mean, why wasn't I interviewed by someone who will actually be in the same building as me? This is all too much to take and I feel like going home. I have been in retail most of my life; retail I can do. I love chatting with people; I class myself as a super-friendly person, and it used to craze the shit out of my husband. Loyal to the end, I had one of those best friends that I thought would always be in my life, but turns out she didn't craze the shit out of my husband and he didn't want to be without her in his life, either – but that's another story.

I've worked in some of Norfolk's shittiest pubs; well, I say some: only a couple stand out – the rest weren't too bad – but not once have I felt like I do now. I'm sweating and my hands are shaking. I want to drive away and say I was feeling unwell or my cat was run over by a huge digger. FYI, I don't have a cat, but it seemed like the logical thing to say in my head. Maybe I'm fooling myself; maybe I can't do this. I've never been an administrator. I'm actually really crap at computers: I wouldn't know where to start. How the hell did I pass that interview?

'No, Ruby,' I tell myself, 'this is not what we do. Now pull up your big girl pants and walk in there. Let's do this, okay?'

One last look in the mirror. I look good for my age – yeah, right, laughs my inner devil. Leaving the car and turning to face what will now be my new place of work, I walk with my head held high into the small white stone building, which looks like a cottage from a movie rather than an office, with small windows on either side of the building, and smaller windows on either side of the door, which is a light shade of blue with a small window near the top. A gold plaque on the door reads 'Hails and Boon, Achieve More Together'. God, I hope it's bigger on the inside.

I walk in and wipe my feet on the welcome mat. I'm standing in a small entrance hall with a white coat-stand directly to my left and a painting of some beautiful white roses hangs on the wall to my right, and this kind of makes me feel calm. This place looks and smells like my home, not your typical office smell. The floor is a dark hardwood and I smell potpourri, a sweet strawberry and vanilla scent. There is a small blue two-seater couch just to the left in front of one of the small windows, with two white fluffy cushions propped up on it. There are a few fashion magazines on a round table in front of the couch, but I notice it's quiet, like really quiet, and I instantly want to play some music to liven the place up.

I walk up to a white desk that is far too neat and tidy for my liking, with a cute little cactus plant sitting in a small pink pot. I can't help but smile and think, 'Oh, how cute'. If it were mine, I would have killed it within a week; but nonetheless cute.

Suddenly, I hear heels on the floor and as I look up, I am looking straight into the face of a very young, well-groomed, very tanned, all-legs, slim-figured woman with the most gorgeous long brown hair and the most perfect white teeth I've ever seen. Told you, I scold myself. Young and twenty something, I'm guessing.

"Good morning, how may I help you?" she says in a very British accent. I instantly think, 'Oh my god, she even speaks likes an angel'; very soft, but very polite – woman crush or what? She must only be in her mid-twenties, and she's wearing the tightest knee-length black dress with a square neckline; a pretty silver necklace that holds a crystal love heart hangs around her perfectly smooth neck, and she looks so elegant – like Audrey Hepburn, *Breakfast at Tiffany's* elegant. Black peep-toe shoes are on her perfect little feet, with red-painted nails poking out; even her toes are elegant.

I feel slightly under-dressed now. I try to straighten my old black jacket that no longer fits me properly – I've even folded the sleeves up because they are too short. I reply in my most polite voice, saying that my name is Ruby Frankton and this is my first day here. I blush, feeling silly around her.

"I mean, I work here." I curse under my breath. "I mean, I'm new here; this is my first day because I'm new here." Why did I make that seem like hard work, ending with an awkward laugh, wishing the floor would swallow me or the building would collapse.

She smiles, saying, "Welcome, Ruby. I'm Celina, and it's a pleasure to meet you," showing me those beautiful teeth again. She really is very pretty. "Please don't be nervous. Let's start with a coffee, shall we?" she says, walking past the desk and into a small kitchen area.

"I'm more of a tea drinker," I reply, "but coffee is fine, thank you." Again, I give another awkward laugh. I must stop doing that.

"So this is the staff kitchen and that's the main office area," she says, pointing back at the desk where

I walked in. "That's where you will be, but you help yourself to coffee or tea whenever you need to. The toilet is just to the left of you" – again pointing past me. "We have three full-time staff working here."

Okay, so she said 'we'; so is she like my supervisor? My head is already trying to analyse everything.

"All the staff are fabulous and super-friendly," she adds, "but I will introduce you to them shortly. Honestly, you will fit right in. They all work in the next room over from where we are now," she says, pointing just past the desk to the left.

Okay, so I'm facing back the way I came in; the toilet is now on my right and the other office-type room is on my left, and the main entrance is straight in front of me. Maybe I should just leg it out of the door and shout, 'Sorry, don't take it personally.'

"It can be a bit full-on sometimes, so you'll be thankful for the peace," Celina says, breaking my thoughts. I can hear a phone ring and low voices and the tapping of keys, and as I peek around the corner I can't really see anything from here. "Then there is another office just off that one which is Mr Hails's office." Okay, so my boss is a man. I breathe out a sigh of relief.

"So, Mr Hails spends, like, all his time in there," she giggles, and continues holding up her perfectly manicured hands. "You will, like, hardly ever see him; he is super-busy and, well, he sort of just lets us get on with it." She giggles again, and I can't help but think, 'Okay, so I'm starting a new job and I'll probably never meet my boss, which is sort of weird but sort of fantastic. I mean, yeah, it would be nice to at least see his face, but if that's how it is, then so be it.'

"Espresso?" Celina asks in a super-happy voice, making me jump.

Oh, crap! No, I hate coffee. "No, thank you," I reply, holding up my own not-so-manicured hands. "I really only drink tea or vodka," I say in an all too geeky voice, and then I give an awkward giggle. Why does she make me feel so nervous?

"Okay," she replies with a big smile, "but I have to say we are fresh out of vodka, I'm afraid, so tea it is." She smiles again.

The kitchen area is just behind the front desk. It's a nice open space and well organised, with a single sink and a state-of-the-art coffee machine, and I'm so glad it provides tea. There are six mugs lined up next to it, like little soldiers; she grabs two and makes me a tea and herself a café latte. There is a fancy wire rack holding all the different kinds of coffee pods – I didn't realise coffee came in so many varieties.

"So, you are responsible for getting milk in for the week," she says. "We will provide you with the account details and the best shop to go to." Great! Now I have extra responsibilities. I barely remember my own milk, let alone milk for lots of other people.

"So, as I said before, your desk is the one where you first came in," she says, breaking my train of thought.

I follow her back to where we started, back to the fancy desk with the cactus. The desk is white and clean; it has two monitors and a white wire-less keyboard with a white matching mouse.

"Oh, I got you this cute little cactus as a welcome gift." She is smiling as she holds it up to me, and I'm thinking, 'Oh, Lord, it's going to die; I'm going to kill it, and you'll hate me.'

But, instead, I smile back and say, "Oh, you shouldn't have done that"; and I think my face must have said it all, because she suddenly asks for my jacket and goes to hang it on the coat-stand in the entrance way. She walks briskly back over to me, all legs and all heels, and I'm feeling really inadequate in my skinny jeans and white pumps.

"Shall me meet the rest of the team, then?" She smiles, walking in the direction of the other room. 'Oh, boy, here we go,' I say to myself, my legs like jelly and my feet feeling as if they are stuck in mud. I'm hopeless at first meetings and I'm always saying the wrong thing, like, all the time, and I want to just run away. I smile and take a deep breath.

Celina walks swiftly into the adjoining room with me in tow, and with a way too happy voice announces my arrival. "Everyone," she says, "this is Ruby Frankton, and this is her first day at Hails and Boon. Can we all make her feel welcome, please?" Wow, I didn't think she would announce it like that, but okay, now I feel even more of a dick – and with that, three chairs spin around to reveal three smiling faces; like I mean really smiling faces. Shit, I think to myself, all eyes on me. Suddenly, I feel very overwhelmed and these people look straight at me, and it's then that I think to myself, 'I really should just leave; I'm not qualified to be here, I'm not qualified to do this job. Why did I even think I could do this job? They will know soon enough and I will have wasted everyone's time. My god, Ruby, calm down, love,' I tell myself in a sarcastic voice.

It's a lovely square room, painted a pale blue, with pictures of fashion adverts hanging on the walls, like some really cool adverts from ripped jeans to prom dresses to shoes, which is kind of cool. I get three hellos, all in sequence, breaking my thought bubble, and all with big wide smiles, and I'm immediately relieved to not have collapsed on the floor in a big fat mess. Maybe it will work out and I can just wing it. 'Okay, Ruby, let's just see how this pans out,' laughs my inner comedian.

I get a few questions thrown at me for the next ten minutes or so, the first being: "Are you married?"

"No," I reply all too quickly. Oh, boy, this is going to be a long story cut short. "Well, yes I was, but we separated five years ago."

One of the men looks at me with an 'oh, you're single' face. "Do you have children?" the same man asks me, smiling.

"Yes, I have two twin girls, Jessica and Belle, who are twenty-three years old.

"Oh, lovely," says Celina. "Where do you come from, then? I mean, has Norwich always been your home?"

"Originally from Sheffield, but moved here to Norfolk for an easier life away from my cheating ex-husband and my backstabbing ex-best friend," and with that I give an awkward 'I don't want to get into details' smile and I think I've said too much. They seem to understand the situation, so don't proceed to ask any further questions about that, and all the time I'm thinking, 'Please let's just move on, please let's talk about anything else.'

"Well, I'm Cecile," says a small-framed woman standing to greet me. "Sorry about all the questions, but we don't often see new faces around the office, and we knew you were coming but we didn't know what to expect." She kind of reminds me of the old lady from *Titanic* who was supposed to be the older version of Rose; but obviously she is only in her early fifties and maybe I was being a little harsh on her. She has light blonde to almost greyish hair that falls in soft wavy curls just to her shoulders. She is rocking some thick-framed glasses and they almost hang off her nose; she's wearing a light beige cardigan and some slim-fitted black jeans. She probably only stands at 5ft 3in tall, but I could see she looked after herself.

I finally say, "Nice to meet you."

Next stands a tall fella. "I'm Mervin," he says in a strong voice as he looks down upon me. He looks like a much younger version of Colin Farrell, maybe early to mid-forties, with curly cropped ginger hair and round spectacles that sit quite broad on top of his long pointed nose, like something from an eighties movie. He's wearing some snazzy light brown corduroy trousers with a black buttoned short-sleeved shirt, and I couldn't help but think, 'Okay, he's a geek.' He has soft hands, so has probably never done a hard day's work in his life, but he seemed lovely and still very energetic in his movements.

"And finally," says Celina, with a twinkle in her eye and a light touch on his arm, "this is Miles"; and I can't help but notice the way she said his name: like she's into him, I mean really into him. She still has her hand on his arm; he doesn't seem to notice, though, or register the fact that she didn't let him say his own name. She looks adoringly at him, like he was her little puppet, or the fact that he looked like he would break if you blew on him. He is a younger-looking lad, probably early twenties, average height, but a very shy manner.

He says, "Hello, nice to meet you," and gives an awkward wave and quickly sits back down. He looks good in dark fitting jeans and Nike Air Max trainers, but I think it's quite funny how scared he looks, yet his t-shirt reads 'No fear'. Actually, he is a very handsome young man; he could use a haircut, of course, but he's got that rough and ready Tom Hardy look to him. I think, 'Oh, bless his soul, he probably just wants us all to go away'; but also I want to tell Celina to let the poor lad speak for himself. Maybe he's used to it. I just wave and say 'hi' back.

"Well," says Celina, clapping her hands, "shall we get you settled in at your desk?"

Out of the corner of my eye, I see a shadow move in the room next to us. I turn to have a better look. I can only hear a low tone of a voice, but I can't make out any words, just a floor-to-ceiling wall of glass and slatted blinds blocking my view. I am very intrigued to see who it is; I can see his shadow and I think at some point I saw the blind move. It is obviously my boss, but he hasn't come out to welcome me, which I think is odd, and a little rude at the same time – but it also kind of makes me feel relieved, because I don't think I can face any more new people today, let alone my boss asking more personal questions.

So we walk back to the first room and I sit at my brand new desk on my brand new chair, about to start my brand new job. I'm staring at my tiny cactus and the computer screen in front of me, and I have no fucking clue as to what I'm doing or why I even applied for this role, and I wonder to myself, 'Is now the time to tell them I can't actually work a pc?'

I quietly giggle to myself, and lean back in my chair, not quite sure as to what to do. Celina tells me she needs to see Mr Hails and leaves me to it. 'Great, now what?' I giggle again, holding my mouth to try and hide the noise. I grab the mouse and the screen comes alive with a bright pink background. I spend some time looking through the many icons, trying to figure what each one means: there are order forms, file after file of pictures, contacts and addresses of our customers, Excel and PowerPoint. I navigate my way through file after file, trying to get my head around how the computer works and why there is no wire to the mouse and what it is we as a company actually do; and all I can figure out is that we pick fashion companies to invest in, or they pick us because they want us to invest in them. These are small companies who are just starting up and that want a better advertisement of their product, like they pay us to make their clothing be the next best thing; so they pay us to make them look good. That's actually quite clever – we have a say in how much of their business we want to invest, and if we see there is a profit through advertising the product, we will invest more, which is kind of cool, but crazy. It's all so over my head. Why would you pay someone to do that sort of thing? Surely you can be like, 'Here is my new sweatshirt, this is what it looks like and this is what it costs'. Well, in my head it seems simple – and then we take a share of the profits for doing some of the hard work. There is lots of advertising involved: making websites, posters and tv ads, and lots of negotiations and agreeing on fees and that sort of thing, which is all, like, way over my head, and the more I think of it the more it gives me a headache. I was grateful to Celina for filling me in before she left to see Mr Hails.

I answer a couple of calls and get to grips with call forwarding, mainly to Cecile, as she seems to be the head of the team and oversees all the decisions before Mr Hails makes the final decision. I'm not totally sure yet what the other guys do. I'm guessing, like, the advertising side of things and designing websites. I bet it's really time-consuming, but also cool. They all seem to have a good bond with each other and are always chatting and laughing and taking the piss out of each other; well, mainly Mervin and Miles, which kind of makes me feel I should be in that room and not stuck out here on my own. My girls are always telling me I have a wicked sense of humour and actually on many occasions I have embarrassed them beyond belief, so why I'm on my own is a mystery to them. The fact is, I can't see me falling in love ever again. I love my own space and my own company, but for the minute, sitting here alone, I just feel awkward, like 'What am I doing here?' awkward. I have still yet to find out what Celina's role is; she seems to be in and out of Mr Hails's office more than anyone else, so maybe they are together or they are related or something, or she could be his personal assistant, like sex-on-tap personal. I smile and crack up on the inside. She doesn't seem to have a desk or do any kind of computer work; she just bounces around the office looking glamorous. Occasionally, when she leaves the office door open, I lean back in my chair to get a glimpse of who I think could be Mr Hails. I see him through the slats – well, his shadow moving around – and I'm taken off to naughty places as to what he might look like. Sometimes I see the outline of him as he stands close to the blind. He looks slim and tall; but as of yet the mysterious man remains unseen. Maybe I should just go pop my head in the door and ask if he would like a coffee, or call him and say, 'Hello, I'm Ruby'; but then again, maybe I should just do my job and stop worrying about it.

Lunch time comes and everyone seems to get up and go out to grab food. Cecile asks me if I would like anything and I say, "No, thank you", holding up my small breakfast bar. Do people not bring their own any more, like I do? It saves money and time, I say to myself; or maybe I'm just getting old. I mean, I am forty-one this year.

While everyone is out, I wander into the other room, eating my cereal bar. I look around the room, and at everyone's desk. Cecile is really untidy, but it looks like organised chaos: papers, folders and files spread out everywhere. I hear music coming from Mervin's computer and I'm shocked when I hear it's the Jonas Brothers – I didn't have him down as a fan of pop music. Instinctively, I start dancing and swaying my hips, really getting into the flow, and as I turn, I see part of a face staring at me through the slats of Mr Hails's office and it stops me in my tracks. Shit, is that my boss? He's on the phone and I think I see him smile. I quickly leave the room all embarrassed, but the rest of the day flies away and by five o'clock everyone starts putting cups in the kitchen and saying their goodbyes. I'm happy it's home time, so I tidy up my desk. I hear idle chit-chat about what everyone's plans are for dinner and so on, and as I'm shutting down my pc, I tell Cecile I will be having a drink tonight to celebrate my new job. I stare at my cactus, mouthing to it, 'Please don't die!' I'm really tired from all the learning of emails and ordering and data, and I need to lay in a hot bath with the biggest glass of vodka and coke I've ever drunk.

As everyone leaves and I shut the door and we all head to the small car park just to the left of the building, scattering like roaches, again I can see what looks like my boss staring out of the window, peeping through the slats like a pervert. Celina appears from nowhere and gets in a very sporty-looking blue Audi. She gives me a wave and I'm guessing she's well in with the boss to have a car like that, or maybe she just works really hard. 'Ruby,' I scoff to myself, 'stop being so judgemental.' Cecile gets in a modest-looking black Volvo and I can see her going home to her Leonardo and feeding all her cats, and I can't help but laugh. She is a lovely person and the kind of woman who I bet has got lots of grandchildren and she spoils them rotten. Mervin hops on a push-bike and, well, it looks like it's seen better days. He slings his backpack over his shoulder – he's probably going home to his gaming pc and a bag of Doritos and dip. Wow, Ruby you are a judgemental bitch today! I'm thinking he lives alone: small flat with one or two close friends that he connects with online; no social life, just work and play – or, Ruby, he's probably married and has four beautiful kids and a stunning wife that gives him a blowjob every morning. I laugh to myself, because I just don't want that image in my head.

And then there was sweet, sweet Miles, who seemed to walk in the direction of the bus, and I think he's probably going home to mummy, having a home-cooked meal and then spending the rest of the night locked in his room, listening to Fall Out Boy and smoking weed out of his bedroom window; or maybe he's not got his licence yet, Ruby, and he's saving hard to be independent so he can finally get a girlfriend, leave his mummy and get laid. I need to stop judging people, I say to myself in the mirror with a smile. I mean, look at me: going home alone.

I start my old banger car and drive home. The roads are quiet; it's early May, so it's just getting dark. My three-bed semi-detached council house is tucked in a corner of a cul-de-sac and both my neighbours are old and don't speak to me, so I don't have to do all that 'hello, how are you?' bullshit. When I finally pull up outside my house, I park my car and head inside. I open the vodka and I call my girls in turn, even though they live together, telling them all about my day, while eating a microwave chicken korma with sticky rice from the freezer. I tell them that I really think I should just quit now as I'm not sure if the job is right for me. I mean, I don't know anything about fashion. I tell them about the other guys in the office, how lovely and welcoming they were, and that the big boss man couldn't be bothered to come say hi. What a dick, I say. Jessica just laughs down the phone at me and tells me to hang in there.

"Not everyone has to rush to meet you, mum," she says. "He must just be really busy and that's why he has Celina to his dirty work for him."

Belle says the same when I call her. She says, "If they don't get your fantastic personality within a few days, then fuck them all!" She laughs loud down the phone. "You can do this, mum; you are a very adaptable person."

They always cheer me up. We have a very close bond and I'm so proud of them both. I tell them that I love them and that I'm going to go drown myself in the bath with my bottle of vodka. They both tell me not to drink too much and that they love me.

"Love you, too," I say back, and I hang up the phone. I head upstairs and into the bathroom. I fill the bath and pour in the bubbles, putting my drink on the side of the bath. I get undressed and step into the water; the bath is hot and the vodka is cold – just the way I like it.

I just can't seem to shake the fact that my own boss didn't come and say hi or want to meet his new receptionist, so to speak; and his eyes looking at me through the slats – what is that all about? The fact he didn't interview me either is just weird; I find it strange and rude, but I got the job, so it can't be all bad. Then I think to myself, 'He's probably really old and short and fat with short grey hair and a double chin, and talks like Dobby from *Harry Potter*.' That made me giggle. Well, whatever he looks like, I'm sure I'll get to meet him at some point.

I finish my drink and I drain the tub, dry myself and dress in my favourite nightie and brush my teeth. My bed has never felt so good and within minutes I'm asleep, dreaming of short bald men and pink cactus plants in pretty pink pots, and the beautiful Celina.

CHAPTER TWO

The alarm wakes me with a start and I instantly roll over and moan to myself that it's too early and I need more sleep; but I get up anyway and slowly dress in my favourite skinny jeans, the only pair of jeans that I feel good in. I have some Crunchy Nut Cornflakes and drink my tea. I brush my teeth and apply my best lipstick, before heading back downstairs to put on my favourite black boots: I have been wearing these boots for over two years and have had them repaired numerous times. I look in the hall mirror before I leave and think, 'Wow, Ruby, you have aged a little in the last five years'; but my hair still looks good — being a natural blonde, not bleached — and it falls in soft curls just to the top of my still pert breasts, and I think, 'Okay, I may have aged, but I still look good.' I may carry a few extra pounds on my hips, but I fit snug in my size 16 skinny jeans, and I'm blessed with being quite tall; I have quite long legs. I'm wearing a light blue long-sleeved shirt and a black lightweight jacket. I feel really good and refreshed and positive, so I walk out of my house and get in my car and drive to work listening to Joe Cocker singing 'You Can Leave Your Hat On', and I feel upbeat and excited for the day ahead.

The drive to Norwich takes me thirty minutes. The weather isn't too bad for early May; even at this time of morning the sun is bright and the air smells fresh, and I'm so glad my drive to work is picturesque and doesn't take an hour like before; and I love the fact that I don't live anywhere near my scumbag ex-husband or my lowlife ex-best friend, and I can drive down the road without passing one of them and thinking, 'I wish I could run them off the road', or go in a shop and know I'm not going to bump into them down the fruit and veg aisle and want to throw a large watermelon at her head – or his, for that matter – and have all that awkward eye contact and me trying not to laugh at her because she thinks she got the man of her dreams, when, in fact, what she got was a balding, overweight, middle-aged man who farts when he sleeps and snores like a train, not to mention the nose picking – it's disgusting! – and, well frankly, he has the passion of a block of hardwood.

I've moved on from all that drama and now I'm looking for peace and quiet. I want to work and look after myself and see my girls every Sunday for a roast dinner and eat shit food and binge-watch tv whenever I want without a man coming in and wanting to watch bloody football, or a nature programme, and have him sit there picking his damn feet and asking me to get him another beer. I want to watch romance and comedies and laugh and be young and play my music loud; and if I don't want to do the bloody housework, I won't bloody do it; and if a man happens to come along, he will live the way I live, because I'm not changing for anyone any more, ever again! This is my time to finally be happy, and anyway, who needs a bloody man? They fucking suck! I would just be happy to find someone I can call when I'm horny and get a quick fix, and then leave.

I pull up at work, lock my car and walk into the office with confidence, and I have a new sense of pride. I get a 'good morning' from everyone while I hang my jacket up, which makes me smile, and I automatically go straight for the coffee machine. Thank god it provides good old English breakfast tea. I stir in my sugar and take a seat at my desk, but just as I sit down, I see who I think is Mr Hails in the other room, and he looks directly at me, tilts his head to one side and smiles. I'm so shocked and embarrassed from yesterday's dancing, I instantly look away. I don't really get a good look at him, but he does look hot from here. Shit! I feel all mushy on the inside.

I turn on my pc and I am ready for the day. I already have five emails – gosh, this computer is more needy than a child – and I work my way slowly through them: mostly people wanting to see Mr Hails for help of some sort. I pop in to see Cecile and get her to help me understand what responses are expected of me and if there is anything they don't want me to say about the company. She is very patient with me and tells me if I'm ever not sure to just forward the email to her and she will deal with it; so we spend the best part of an hour going through files and contacts. She tells me I will have to try and touch base with some of our existing clients, as we haven't had a receptionist for over a month and they will love that we call and check how things are going. I see the slats are open to Mr Hails's office and I can see a figure sitting at his desk; he is rotating idly on his chair and he is on the phone. When his chair comes back towards the office, he stops when he sees me and puts his head to one side and smiles again. I quickly turn away and tell Cecile I need to return to my work. I'm more confident now and feeling a bit more helpful and that I've achieved something, so when my phone rings I automatically pick it up and say, "Hello, Hails and Boon, how can I help you?"

A male voice on the other end speaks with a soft tone, and with a hint of sarcasm he says, "Hi, with whom am I speaking?"

I reply in a friendly voice, "This is Ms Frankton."

"I see," says the voice on the other end. "I'm guessing you're the new receptionist, Ms Frankton," he continues.

"Oh, um, I would say more like the administrator," I tell him without thinking. Why the hell would he want to know this, and why didn't I just say yes?

"I see; and how do you like being an

administrator?" he asks in a cocky kind of way.

"I seem to be getting the hang of things and the staff are lovely and very patient with me," I say. "I don't mean to be rude, but is there something I can help you with?" I continue.

"No, no," he says. "I'm so sorry to take up your time, Ms Frankton," he adds. "Now, do tell me, what's the boss like?" he asks me in a strange, playful voice. He has got me puzzled. What an odd question, I think. "I hear he's a bit of a dick," he adds.

"Well, to be honest," I reply, "I've not met him or spoken to him yet, and yeah, as far as a boss goes, I think he's been a bit strange and, well, rude," and I'm thinking, I like this person. "I'm presuming he's far too busy to waste his time seeing little old me," I say with a sigh.

"I see," he replies. "Well, how about you just go and introduce yourself and say hi," he adds.

"Well, yeah, I could do that, but I think it would be rude to just go and knock on his door and be, like, 'Oh hi, I'm Ruby, oh, and I think you're weird'!" I laugh.

"I see," says the mystery man, and I'm starting to wonder who this man is.

"I'm sorry to ask again, but is there anything I can help you with?" I say, feeling a bit guilty for calling my boss rude and weird.

"Well, Ms Frankton, how about you grab a cup of tea and come to my office and let's see how much time we can waste together and maybe see just how rude I can be."

Shit, fuck, bollocks! I freeze instantly, not knowing what to say. Shit, shit, shit! It's the boss man himself! Day two, and I'm already in trouble. Why didn't I look who was calling? Jesus, Ruby; shit, what do I do, what do I say? Nothing – you don't say anything; let him do all the talking. Just calm yourself down. "Well, it would be lovely to meet you, Mr Hails. I'll be through shortly and yes, lovely, I'm on my way," I can't help but stutter. Fuck, shit, bollocks! Why, Ruby, why do you say these things?

I hang up the phone in such a way that it falls off the base, and I press a few buttons that seem to speed dial a random number and I quickly hang up and curse myself for being so clumsy, and I instantly want to cry. What have I said? Nothing, Ruby, calm the fuck down. Could he tell I was just being playful? He started it anyway. Should I have been more professional? Yes, I should have. My head is a mushy mess, but I gather my thoughts, make a cup of tea and head to his office. Standing at the door for what seemed an age, I think of what to say: just play it cool. I straighten up and take a deep breath, and hold my mug for support. I should just say hello and be natural, or say, 'Hey, how's things?' No, you fucking idiot, you can't say that! I breathe back out again. Just carry on and be yourself.

I clear my throat and knock, then enter the office,

which is a pretty cool place. It smells divine: the fragrance of aftershave and hair gel mixed with fresh linen. There is a lovely old deep red recliner in the right-hand corner, next to a beautiful oak bookcase filled with old and new books. On the wall straight ahead are three beautiful black and white pictures of a construction site – I'm guessing in the early twenties and thirties London. He himself is sitting at a big oak desk to the left of me, with a state-of-the-art computer system and monitors in every direction. Behind him is a matching oak desk with some gadgets and random wooden puzzles on top and a cool Newton's cradle.

I look over at him as he looks up and say, "Hello, Mr Hails, it's nice to finally meet you," as I walk over with my hand held out. Crap, was I sounding pissy! I didn't mean for it to sound like that, but after a second he gets up from his deep red obviously expensive office chair and walks towards me with his arm outstretched, and it's then that I finally get to see his beautiful face – and when I say beautiful, I mean, oh my fucking god, this man is sex-on-legs drop-dead gorgeous! He is Ryan Reynolds, Ryan Gosling and Bradley Cooper all rolled into one sexy beast, with short dark cropped hair messily brushed over to one side and the brightest blue eyes I've ever seen, and a beautiful jawline that puts Matt Bomer to shame. He makes what sounds like a sigh and shakes my hand, and wow, he has soft hands, but still very strong – the kind I want to run up the inside of my thigh and gently stroke my most delicate parts. He hold my hand for far longer than I was comfortable with, then asks me to have a seat, and immediately I'm thinking, 'Fuck, this is it and he's going to tell me off. Oh, yes please, sir, smack me hard on my soft plump buttocks!' Then I think, 'Jesus, Ruby, get a grip', so I quite clumsily sit in one of the two single dark red leather chairs facing his desk and my heart is racing and I think I'm going to throw up, or I'm thinking I want to throw myself at him and ride him like a train. Oh my god, Ruby, stop it, he's your boss – yeah, but goddamn look at him, he's fucking hot!

Once seated, I quickly say, "I'm sorry for what I said on the phone."

He returns to his desk and sits back in his own chair and looks at me with what appears to be confusion, or maybe he's just sussing me out to see how I react to his beautiful face. I stare right back at him and, I mean, I could sit and stare all day. He sucks in his bottom lip and oh, wow, I didn't notice that mouth – that's a kissable mouth; he has lovely lips that I want to chew on! Ruby Frankton, stop it now, or so help me god…, I scold myself.

Then he finally speaks. "Its fine. I was only messing with you."

"Oh my god, really?" I say, feeling relieved and placing my hand on my chest. He had sounded pissed, I thought.

"So how did you find your first day?" he asks, amused, and I know he's referring to the dancing. Now, is he asking me because he genuinely wants to know, or is he saying, 'I hope you say you liked it so I can give you a disciplinary'? Oh god, yes, discipline me, Mr Hails, I giggle to myself.

I bite hard on my top lip and all I can say is, "Fine," in a high-pitched 'I feel really awkward and horny all at the same time' voice. I place my cup on the small round table between the chairs and put my hands between my legs, as I'm not sure what else to do with them. He watches me closely, following my hands. I know he wants more, because he leans forward, resting his chin on his right fist; so I continue and say, "It was really good, thank you. I learned a lot from Cecile, and I would like to thank you for giving me this opportunity to work for you… I mean, your company," I stutter again.

He smiles ever so slightly. Why is he smiling at me? Oh god, what's he thinking? He's fucking sexy, what the actual fuck – do people actually look like this? He then asks me if I've ever worked in an office before or if I know anything about fashion, or if, in fact, I actually know anything about his company, again with that slight smile. He knows; yep, he knows I have zero experience, and he knows I have no clue who he is, let alone who Boon is. I feel silly and he's laughing at me, not on the outside, but he's laughing all right, so I sit up straight and I say, "No, I've never worked in an office, but I've dealt with tough customers before, when I was a supervisor, and I've broken up lots of fist fights in bars, if that helps," and I can't help but do an awkward chuckle, all the while thinking, 'There, take that; I'm tough and I can take you on, or I could take you to bed and do really rude things to you!' I can't help but smile, but why, oh why, Ruby, didn't you just give a short answer of no, just no? My inner teenager is curling up with embarrassment, but his smile gets bigger and he relaxes more into his chair.

"So you worked in the pub industry?" he asks. Oh, he wants to know about me, and this makes me cringe.

"Yes," I say. "I worked in a few bars in and around Sheffield for the best part of seven years before I became the assistant manager at a local supermarket." Feeling happy with my answer, I flick the right side of my hair back over my shoulder and he's watching me very closely.

"I see," he says. "So what made you decide to work in fashion and do something you really don't seem to know anything about?"

And there it is, the straight to the point, 'What the fuck are you doing here, Ruby?' question. Oh, I see how it is, I think to myself: he's looked me up and down and decided because I dress the way I do that I'm not into fashion. Jesus, look at that lot out there! He's making me mad. "So you think, just because I can pull a pint and I break up big scary men from silly little fights, that I've got no brain?" I say in a pissed voice. I can see he's trying to beat me down – oh lord, yes, please, beat away, beat me into submission! Stop it, Ruby, and answer the damn question properly. I take a deep breath and say in a stronger, more independent voice, "My soon to be ex-husband decided my now ex-best friend was the woman for him" – irrelevant, I know, but I keep going – "so he moved her into our marital home and I needed to move out and move away. It's as simple as that. I wanted a new challenge and, given time, I will excel at that challenge. I'm good with numbers and I can read and write. Now surely, in today's market, that should be good enough." I breathe out and, sitting up straight in my chair, I feel more confident than ever.

Meanwhile, he remains silent – he hasn't moved for over five minutes. He really is very good looking, and he has that jawline I want to run my tongue along and that mouth – well, it's just calling me to kiss him, and kiss him I want to; I want to know what he tastes like. I am jolted out of my deep state of lusting when the door suddenly swings open and makes us both jump, and in walks Celina. She looks amazing in her long grey pencil skirt and white ruffled blouse, with ridiculous heels that seem to be far too high for an office job – but god, they look good on her. Her hair is up in a tight bun and she has the brightest red lipstick on. She smells of sweet cherry perfume, and, well, I suddenly feel very inadequate.

I rise from my chair and grab my cup and start for the door, when Mr Hails speaks quite abruptly. "Celina, I was in the middle of talking with Ms Frankton," he snaps. Oh, he sounds pissed, but his voice is still calm and sexy. Oh lord, when he says my name like that, I just want to rip his clothes off and eat him all up. I blink at Celina and can't help but feel bad for her as she seemed so happy to see him, but she quickly apologises and walks back out and closes the door behind her.

I look at him wide-eyed and in total bewilderment, and say, "I really should be getting back to work," not really knowing what my next move should be, and not that I want to move or leave his office, but I really can't stay in here all day, unless he wants to strip me naked and throw me on the recliner – oh, what a lovely thought! I try and hide my smile by sucking in both my lips and breathing in. He puts his hands in his pockets and looks at me with those sexy eyes I could melt into, and I'm automatically drawn to his crotch, and I know as soon as I'm looking at his manhood that he's looking at me, watching my reaction, and when we lock eyes, I turn the brightest shade of pink. I just want to run and hide under my desk, but instead, I look straight back at his bright blue eyes all flushed, and say my really pathetic, "Thank you for wasting some of your time on me and goodbye, Mr Hails," and as I leave the office I feel his eyes on me. Really, Ruby, that was all you can say: a thank you and goodbye? I slap my own forehead with my palm as I walk away, but he calls after me and I turn.

"Good to meet you, Ms Frankton. I'm happy to waste time with you whenever you're free." He shows me that sexy smile again as he steps back and closes his door. Wow, I think in my head, just wow!

Back at my desk, I sit and I'm silent, just staring at my cactus – and all I can think about is his beautiful face and that beautiful smile and his beautiful hands and where he can put those beautiful hands; and that comment about me wasting his time, what was that all about?

"I could waste a lot of time doing things to that man, Ruby," says Cecile, waking me from my sexual daydream. "Did you see that email from Runaway Lingerie about our scheduled meeting next Friday?" She smiles kindly. "It's just this is kind of a big deal," she says.

"Yes," I reply. "Sorry, I was miles away."

"Marisa la Claire said they would be here at 9.30am sharp and they really look forward to meeting with us all. We are a team," Cecile says, "and we are in this together," she chants all preacher-like.

Wow, I've never really been part of a team before; usually, it's all bitches out for themselves. It feels nice and it feels comfortable. We get through the rest of the day in a peaceful banter between offices kind of way and there seems to be a lot of sexual talk between Miles and Mervin; well, I say talk, more like taking the piss out of each other's non-existent sex life, which just confirms my earlier thoughts.

Mervin is constantly saying, "Miles, your mum's hot."

While he replies, "Yeah, that's what I told your mum this morning when my dick was in her mouth."

But they are a good bunch and I'm really starting to settle; it's only day two and I feel I've been here forever.

Celina has disappeared again. God knows what she does all day; maybe she doesn't actually work here and she is Mr Hails's girlfriend. But then I think no, because of the way she was with Miles, or maybe she just wants to be near Mr Hails all the time, even if he does scold her like that. Maybe it's her way of getting higher in the company; I mean, I bloody well would – I would like totally want to sit on his face twenty-four seven, I giggle in my head. So I've been on my own for a while, a girl can dream.

I eat my lunch and print off some letters for Cecile, then I organise some catering for next week's meeting: I call the local hotel and spa, who are super-helpful. They ask me what sort of food we would like and I tell them that I have no idea what people like to eat these days, so I just go by what I would like to eat and throw in some vegetarian choices and some gluten-free for luck; plus, I have no idea how many people will be joining us – Cecile thinks at least three from Runaway Lingerie, so that's nine of us all together; okay, we will go with nine, and I've noted all allergies and preferences. There are far too many allergies out there, so best to be safe than sorry. I ask Cecile if anyone in the office has any allergies and she shrugs her shoulders as if to say, 'I don't think so.' The hotel says it can be delivered on the Friday morning just after eight-thirty, which is perfect for me.

It's soon the end of the day and I don't see or hear any more from the sex god Mr Hails, and I can't wait to talk to my girls and tell them all about my day. I've been on my own for over five years now, so any kind of an encounter with a sex-god-looking man like Mr Hails has to be shared.

We all say our goodbyes and head for the car park.

CHAPTER THREE

Once I'm home, I pour the vodka and put on my favourite playlist of mixed eighties music and eat some leftover pasta from the fridge. I call my girls and tell them the gossip; they love hearing all about the beautiful Mr Hails, and how he must be this super-rich Mr Grey type, and I laugh and say, 'if only!' We could all use one of them in our lives, I laugh. We chat for an hour; they tell me about their flatmate who is so messy and unclean, and I laugh and say, "Well, if that's all you have to worry about, I'd be grateful. I'm just happy to get you both in the same room at the same time for a chat." I tell them I love them and then we say our goodbyes.

I put some washing on and head up to clean my teeth. I wonder what Mr Hails is doing right now? I bet he's all wet and glossy from having a shower, and I bet he works out naked in his bedroom. No, Ruby, he's probably still at work and totally not thinking of you; and anyway, it's only saddos like me that go to bed at 9.30pm, and I know my thoughts are right: I am sad. I'm set in my ways and my body is showing some signs of wear and tear. I'm tired, but feeling good about the future, and I just want to do well at my new job. I climb into bed and set my alarm.

The rest of the week flows pretty easily and I'm getting the hang of what is expected of me; it's pretty simple really, just answer the phone and reply to emails, set up meetings and organise food when needs be. Ordering office supplies is a daily thing – I'm always getting requests for this and that – and organising maintenance when things go wrong. We have a delivery of coffee and tea on Thursday, which, believe it or not, is one of the highlights of my week. The other was meeting the sexy beast. The others tease me about drinking so much tea, but I really don't mind; they are a good laugh.

When it's finally Friday, I'm excited it's one hour till I can go home and I can't wait for Saturday to go clothes shopping – I need a new wardrobe and fast. I'm going to get some new office clothes and I'm hoping to dress to impress, not that Mr Hails would even notice, let alone care; but I can't seem to shake him off my mind. The possibilities are endless, and I've thought of his naked body next to mine on more than one occasion – well, who wouldn't when you know an Adonis is only a few feet away from you and you can't touch it? But if he does see me I will look damn good and maybe buy some new underwear just for luck. 'For fuck's sake, Ruby,' I scold myself. 'Really, he's not going to want you.'

I stand in the kitchen, making my last cup of tea for the day. I'm dressed in my best skinny jeans and

I'm suddenly aware of the door opening. I turn to see who it is, and it's Mr Hails walking in, talking on his phone. I stand and stare, because he's just so fucking sexy. He sees me, stops talking and smiles. "You look very nice today, Ms Frankton," he says, and then starts talking on the phone again and walks away, still smiling at me. Holy Jesus fuck, did he just say that? Oh my Lord, how can a man make us feel that way? I should have said something back, but I was lost in the moment.

I have ended my week on a high, so with Saturday morning done and dusted, I'm back home with the girls, going through my new wardrobe.

"Wow, mum, that's a lot of sexy clothes," says Belle. "Oh my god," she says, totally bemused, "you got yourself some new boots!"

"They are black leather lace-up ankle boots," I say with a wicked grin.

"I love them, mum! Look at the heels on those bad boys – you're going to look super-hot!" she continues with a big grin and a giggle.

"He has to give you a bonus just for looking sexy," says Jessica. She is being way too playful, but I smile and hug my new clothes like an excited schoolgirl getting her first crush.

We spend the rest of the day chatting and chilling in the garden. The sun is warm for May, but soon enough it's time for them to leave.

"We will see you tomorrow, mum. Don't forget

the sprouts this time!" shouts Jessica, as they climb into Belle's beloved Mini.

"I won't," I shout. "Love you, guys." We all wave and they drive away, so the house is once again quiet. I put some washing away and go up to bed.

Monday comes all too quick and I'm up extra early and ready for the day. I've straightened my hair and I'm wearing my new Jimmy Choo perfume – I look and feel like a million dollars. I've shaved all vital parts and I've got on my best underwear. I treated myself to a pair of air pods that everyone keeps raving about, just because I can; it's nice not having someone making me feel bad for treating myself. I must say the sound quality is amazing, and listening to Dire Straits on repeat, singing along to 'Money for Nothing' is awesome. I'm even taking them to work so I can listen to music through my lunch break, as sometimes it's just too quiet; even with the banter, there seems to be way too many quiet moments, and I've not plucked up the courage to ask for a radio.

Leaving the house, I climb into my car and hit the dual carriageway, weaving in and out of the traffic. The sun is up and it's going to be a beautiful day. I pop to the shop and collect some milk for the week ahead. The office is super-quiet when I arrive, but Miles comes out to talk to me, which he never does, and says everyone has come down with the sickness bug, so it's just me and him. "Oh," I say, "great." I dressed up for nothing and I think I look super-hot and I'm just going to sit here all day and be bored. "Oh well," I say, "we can still have a good day, hey, Miles?"

He smiles and walks back to his desk. Okay, maybe not.

The morning seems to drag on forever. "God, I'm so bored," I say, after another hour of swinging around on my chair and making yet another cup of tea. No one to talk to or look at; Miles is just huddled over his desk. 'Great fun you are,' I moan under my breath. After another hour of searching up random names on social media and trying to stalk some ex-school friends, as well as ex-bosses, I decide to have lunch early. I even decide to walk into town: it's only a few minutes, and the day is warm and the streets alive with people. There is live music in the main market place, and the smell of food fills my nose. I grab a club sandwich from my favourite deli with a can of cold Fanta, and walk back to the office with my music in my ears. I can't help but feel happy with a hand full of fizzy and a chocolate muffin. 'Romeo and Juliet' is playing softly in my ears as I push open the office door and practically stumble in the entrance way backwards and into a solid object. I turn and immediately I'm face to face with Mr Hails. I stop and just stare, looking into his cool blue eyes. I feel myself blush as he looks me dead in the eye – and oh my Lord, he smells divine! I can smell his aftershave and

I know it's Joop. I'm all a mess and heavy breathing, while he looks delicious, and I have to fight not to jump on him there and then. I freeze when he raises his right hand and takes one of the pods from my ear and places it in his own, the whole time never breaking eye contact. The music continues just as Mark Knopfler sings 'When we make love you used to cry', and I'm so lost in the moment I don't realise my mouth is drooping wide open and I think I'm drooling. He just stares back at me all calm and sexy-looking, while my heart is beating out of my chest and I'm hardly breathing. He smiles, puts his right index finger under my chin and gently closes my mouth. We are so close and his touch does things to my insides. Then he places the pod from his ear back into mine, never taking his eyes off me and never saying a word, and then slowly steps to the side so I can pass, and when I move, he watches me with a slight grin and an unspoken word of acceptance to me being in the exact same place at the exact same time as him, and I feel oddly calm, and yet the whole situation is unreal; and just like that, he turns and walks out the door and disappears, and I'm left feeling in awe of what just happened.

I don't move for what seems an age. I feel total lust for a man I barely know and I just stand there, breathing in and out as if I were a robot, and I'm all foggy and there is a screaming inside my brain to go after him and ask him a question, any old question, just so I can look at his beautiful face a little longer and hear his voice once again. But I don't do that. I simply turn, walk to my desk and sit down. I can't comprehend what's just happened. Why did he not speak? Why did I not speak? Why does he smile at me that way? And I can't help but feel like a small child lost at the park.

Wednesday comes around and the team are back at work. I'm so relieved to see everyone and have a normal conversation; bless Miles for trying to make small talk with me at the coffee machine, asking me about the weather or if I've ever in actual fact seen a baby pigeon, but I'd rather talk to another female about anything else other than the weather or a bloody pigeon. Sometimes, we just need other women around to chat shit to; women get other women, men just know about men and sport, and how big their dicks are. It's that simple.

Celina swoons in, but only to grab some envelopes from Cecile, and they kiss each other on the cheek all French like; then she heads back towards me. "Good morning, Ruby," she says, walking past my desk. "You look lovely today." Then she exits just as fast, while I look down at my plain skinny jeans and my old faithful white woollen sweater and think, 'Wow, she really was being polite. I really do look shit today.' I really need to find out what her job title is; it's bugging me.

This week has again flown by and I don't know

where the time goes. I've not seen Mr Hails since Monday, and I know with this meeting looming I'm getting more and more anxious to see him, so I need to pick my best outfit. 'My god, Ruby, listen to yourself! He's probably married and has kids, or he's sunning himself every weekend on a yacht in Italy with the stunning Celina; plus, he's obviously younger than you, and, well, look at him: he's a god and you're a middle-aged overweight divorcee with a bad diet and just as bad taste in men.' Okay. Okay, I tell myself, let's just see how it pans out; and my inner voice just laughs. 'Let's face it, Ruby, most of my let's-see-if-it-pans-out have worked so far, but I think this one will be different.'

Friday is here and I'm super-excited. I've never really been in any meetings of this type before and I'm dressed in some new dark blue skinny jeans and a white ruffled blouse and a black woollen waistcoat. I feel good, even if I don't look it. This meeting thing is all new to me; my life is so sad. Shawn Mendes's 'Mercy' is playing on the stereo on the way to work, and I sing along like the popstar I'm not. I've picked up some more milk from the local one-stop shop. I park in the car park, lock my car and walk in. I'm forty-five minutes early and find the door open, so I enter quietly and I can see its only Mr Hails's office light on, so I creep in like a naughty eighteen-year-old doing the walk of shame. I do not want to be heard, as I really can't face him yet, and I need to get the meeting room set up, which is just the main office with a few extra tables and chairs being brought in and put together to look more fancy; but I still need it to look nice and professional.

The food arrives just after eight twenty-five, and I put as much of it as I can in the small kitchen fridge. There are a dozen fresh croissants and a variety of bagels and buns with jams, cream cheese and marmalade for breakfast, then thick-cut sandwiches, a variety of pies and sausage rolls for lunch, fresh fruit with crisps and cookies – so really it's just your basic kids' party food; but breakfast looks really good.

Before I can finish setting up and putting the coffee pot and mugs on the table, I am fully aware Mr Hails's office door has opened and he walks right up behind me. I feel his warm body close to mine and I feel his breath on my neck and I freeze. I can smell his aftershave, that sweet, sweet smell of Joop – it's such an erotic smell. I try to carry on, but every time I try to move, I feel my legs go to jelly and I have visions of him pushing me down on the table and taking my jeans down to my ankles and taking me from behind in a crazed frenzy, him pulling my hair and me arching my back in pleasure so he can kiss my neck. Oh, if only – but instead he reaches around me in a slow seductive manner, fully aware of what he's doing. "Good morning, Ms Frankton," he says, all sexy, and I can feel his forearm brush the edge of mine and the hairs on my arms all stand to attention.

The air is electric, as he grabs a mug and then fills it with coffee, while all the time I do not speak; it's like a secret game between us, and I swear he is smiling that beautiful smile, but I dare not look, because I'm shaking like a leaf. He strides back to his office and I can't help but turn my head to watch; he has the best looking arse I've ever seen, so tight in his silky grey trousers. My god, I want to grab that arse! He stops in the doorway, turns towards me, smiles – like, I mean, a wicked smile, enough to make a grown woman come in her undies smile – and he slowly shuts the door. I am floored. He is playing a very seductive game with me and I love it. I'm thinking it's go time; if he wants to play, then let's play. I'm not sure what that means yet, as I've been single for some time and I don't know how to flirt, but I'll do my best – and let's be honest, my own arse is probably one of my best features, so maybe I can use that against him in some way.

Eight fifty-five arrives and we all gather in the office for a quick brief before Runaway Lingerie arrive. I'm standing at the back of the room, trying to hide, and now and again I lock eyes with Mr Hails, and he has that look of pure sexiness on his face, but not in the way of 'Oh, look at me.' He's very humble-looking; he half-smiles and it sends my mind into overdrive. God, I want to grab hold of him and do things I've only ever dreamed of.

Cecile talks about the company called Runaway

Lingerie. Marisa la Claire, who has over ten years' experience in the lingerie industry, would like to expand her business and aim for a wealthier sector, but needs our help to come up with some ideas and advertisements to promote her new range – they have their own sexy new line that they want us to invest in. They seem to have come up against a brick wall with online sales, and our aim is for their naughty but nice collection to be the main topic for today. It's very good quality lingerie, but sales have just dropped off. The new line will be a new start, and they need our help to get them back on their feet; they feel it's not been advertised in the right way so far, and that's why they have reached out to us.

"Mr Hails has invested a lot of time and money on this; he has spent many nights here, ironing out the fine details, so let's do him proud and let's not waste any time getting this right." And when she says 'waste', he looks right at me and I blush. "So let's get some ideas flowing and get something down on paper, and let's make this new adventure shine. Oh, and let's have a productive day."

Wow, it all sounds fantastic and everyone is pumped. Three representatives join us at nine thirty. Marisa la Claire is a very stern-looking woman with short black hair. She does not seem to wear much make-up and her sense of style is not to be desired – I for one would not wear a pair of overalls that look like I fell into several tins of paint. She has two other women with her, both looking as equally dull as the other.

We all have coffee and some breakfast while doing the mindless chit-chat of hellos and how are you. Well, the boys tuck into breakfast anyway – they can eat for England.

Runaway Lingerie's new line is colourful, with some pretty out-there prints, aiming at the average slim-food cautious fanatic, and I think, 'Great, yet again another sexy set of underwear for the skinny people to look good in; what about us larger women who struggle to find a decent bra that actually fits us properly?'

Three hours in and we are going strong. The breakfast foods have all but gone, and we have some good ideas. I sit jotting down notes and taking a genuine interest in what's being said, and the boys come up with some good catchy lines; but, of course, the main focus is on being naughty but nice. Celina is a pro at talking the talk: she just flows into it, and wow, does she have a good imagination. I'm starting to see what it is she does best; she could sell ice to an Eskimo.

Come two o'clock, we stop for lunch, which Cecile helps me serve. I head back to the kitchen to make myself a tea and Mr Hails walks straight up to me at the coffee machine. My god, he is sexy, and my god, he looks good. He is toned and slim, just a bit taller than me; his white shirt is unbuttoned at the top so I can just about see his beautiful neck and what I think is a hint of a tattoo. It's Trible looking, but I can't be sure. He asks me what I think so far, and am I keeping up, the smug bastard, and why I've not spoken a word all morning, and he says someone with a beautiful voice like mine should be heard. Wait, what, he thinks I have a beautiful voice, the voice in my head laughs loudly.

"I for one think you have a lovely voice," he adds. "Oh, and you look good today." And with that, he picks up a grape and pops it in his beautiful mouth and starts rolling it around on his tongue, and I can't stop looking at his mouth and his soft full lips. I just want to bite his bottom lip hard and I want him to kiss me so badly; I want his tongue all over me. "Plus," he finally says, "I think you would look good in something naughty."

My mouth drops open and I stutter, "I'm listening and taking notes." My god, I sound like a dork. 'I'm listening and taking notes'? What a crock, I scoff. With that, he smiles and walks away. Yes, that's right, you walk away, you sexy beast. Oh, how I love to watch you walk away! This beautiful man is driving me crazy.

Back in the meeting, we start to slow down with the ideas and we start to wrap things up. Everyone seems happy with the plan of action, but then Mr Hails suddenly stands up and puts his hands in his pockets. "Thank you, everyone, for your input today," he says, "but I think Ms Frankton has got something she would like to say." Then he looks straight at me and smiles, and in that moment I lock eyes with him and give him a stare of utter shock. I want to throw something at him, something big and heavy, and I want to run away. He looks straight back at me with his wicked smile and sits back down, while I instantly go cherry red as all eyes are on me. OH, MY GOD, I think I'm going to hurl. I tell them that I really don't have anything important to say. I can't breathe.

"Come on," says Celina, "we would love to hear it. Don't be shy, we are all friends here," she adds.

As I stand up and prepare to talk, Mr Hails shouts, "Why don't you come over here, Ms Frankton?"

I stop and look directly at his grinning face. I know what he's doing, the sexy bastard. I move slowly to the front of the room, and I have to squeeze past Mr Hails, saying "Excuse me" in a piss-taking way, so that I am next to where he's sitting. I can't help but want to slap his face as I walk past, but I'm fully aware that my plump behind is now right in his eyeline, and this makes me smile on the inside, because I know he's looking – I can feel it. I clear my throat and say, "Hi." My hands are shaking. "I really love all your ideas, they are super-fantastic, and thank you so much for letting me have my say." I turn to Mr Hails when I say it, as he's the one who put me in the spotlight. Not one person speaks, and I can see everyone is holding their breath, waiting patiently. Mr Hails is still full-on smiling, and it's putting me off. I clench my own hands and squeeze them together to stop them shaking, and for the next five minutes I stutter and stumble on about how the whole lingerie range in general doesn't seem to cater for us larger-boned people, women in particular, and all the adverts you see are of younger, very slim women who, well, make any underwear look good, and I mean, yeah, its aim is to get people to look at the advert and say, 'Wow, look how good she looks in that beautiful bra with matching briefs. I simply must get up off the couch and exercise to look like her.'

"Let's show the beautiful women lying on the sand in their tiny bikinis. I mean, come on, it just looks false; it's not like that for us in the real world. People who want to look sexy and who want to buy underwear won't go to she shops; they will buy online, because we don't want to be made to feel fat and ugly by the skinny bird serving us. Most larger women want or need to cover their lumpy bits, and seeing adverts or posters with slim women looking all fab won't make us want to go out and buy it. We need to feel that what we put on has got our back kind of thing; what we wear should be comfortable but sexy, and we should not have to worry about looking fat. So why not show real women in real lingerie, looking real, if you get my meaning." My hands are all sweaty and I just want to leave. I finish with a thank you and a kind of head bow, then turn to look at Mr Hails, who is still smiling, so I must have done something right, or I've just amused him in some way.

Marisa la Claire jots something down and stands. She says thank you to us all, and confirms with everyone that it has been a very productive meeting and she can't wait to see the end results and get some feedback on ways they can improve. She comments on the food options and nods towards me and says it was a good selection, to which I smile and say, "Thank you; please feel free to take some for your journey home,"

Mr Hails gets up to shake hands and he is so close to me; and I know he's doing it on purpose. Feeling overwhelmed, I make my move. I need to get out of this room. I can hear everyone start chatting at the same time, so I slide out of the room and away from Mr Hails's ever-watching eyes and off to the bathroom. I need to get away from him. Never in my life have I felt so flustered. I feel like crying. I walk past the kitchen area and through a door just to the left, where a small corridor leads into a communal bathroom. This is a very feminine bathroom considering it's for all to use; the toilet is opposite the door, and the sink is on the left, with a small cabinet underneath. We have pink hand towels hanging on a rail next to the sink, and a pink rug in the shape of a flower on the floor, with pictures of pink flowers on the wall. Even the soap is pink passionfruit! It's very clean and smells very sweet. There is no window, yet it feels very open and light, with white walls.

I spend a few minutes catching my breath and getting my heart to stop beating so fast. I wash my hands and look into a small round mirror just above the sink. 'Well done, Ruby,' I chant, 'you did damn good.' But my god, what the hell was he playing at? He knew damn well I was uncomfortable up there.

I dry my hands and fold the hand towel back on the rail and open the door and walk right into Mr Hails. "Oh, shit!" I say, all arms and chest and clumsiness. "Sorry, I didn't see you there." I want to leave, but he's just not moving; he is grinning, and with his body full of sexiness, just stands there, looking deep into my eyes. He steps forward, pushing me back into the bathroom, and the door shuts behind him, so that we are now closer than ever in this small space, and that Joop smell fills my senses, and my god, I want him to take me now in this tiny space; I want him to kiss me so bad I think at one point I even said it out loud. I want him to touch me so badly.

He moves forward so I have to step around him, trying to slide away, and my back is now against the closed door. He steps forward, placing his left hand on the wall beside me, and, looking into my eyes, he leans forwards and whispers in my ear, "Maybe I was trying to sneak up on you, Ms Frankton." He is so close, I can feel his hair on my cheek. I'm frozen and I can't breathe. "Maybe I want to be here now with you," he whispers, looking into my eyes, and if I was to move just an inch our lips would be touching. I can feel his breath on my face and I don't understand why he just doesn't kiss me and get it over and done with; but I know it's all a game.

I try to turn around to grab the door handle, pushing myself against him on purpose, and he smiles; but in the same sense I want to get away from him and, oh, I don't know what I want – I just know I want him to kiss me. He is basically pressed against me, and we are here now in this moment, the heat between us intense. I try to suck in my stomach, but that only pushes out my breasts even more and I know he felt them on his chest, because he gives me another smile, as if to say, 'I know what you're trying to do'; like the kind of smile that just screams, 'I'm so going to fuck you, and fuck you I will' – and in that moment I know it to be true. He stands back ever so slightly and I make my move; like a squirming snake, I wriggle away from him, saying that I must get back. I leave the bathroom and head back to the main office, where everyone is packing up, ready to leave.

I'm not really sure as to what just happened, or how I really feel about it. I know I feel hot and I ache between my legs, and I need to get home to a huge glass of vodka. I start to clean up the mess and put the cups in the kitchen sink. My head is all a-flutter and I'm just moving like a robot, trying not to break anything. Mr Hails comes from the bathroom and walks past me, but doesn't look at me. 'Oh, nice,' I yell in my head, 'now he's ignoring me' – another game he likes to play. Well, I don't care, so how about that? But I do care. I care a lot, and I care what I might do next or what he might push me to do. I swear to god, this weekend will be torture for me now because I'm sexually frustrated and I need him between my legs and I damn well need his mouth on mine. I need him to put me out of my misery and just kiss me, and kiss me hard. This is so unfair! I wonder if he's done this to anyone else, and maybe that's why I'm the new receptionist, because he shagged the last one and she became too needy. Oh god, am I the next victim?

We all say our goodbyes and Celina says well done on a good day. As we exit the building, only Mr Hails remains. I feel sad to be going home alone, but also relieved, because I need to talk with my girls and get my head straight, and I'm glad the journey home doesn't take forever, because I just want to get in a nice hot shower and wash the smell of Joop from my mind. He's got me good, he's got me hooked. I don't want to lose my job, but in the same breath I need the danger and the excitement, because what's life without a little danger? But I need to think clearly about every move I make from now on, so I come to the decision that I'm going to play along, but I'm going to keep him at arm's length. I'm going to be professional, and keep it friendly; yes, that's right, we can be friends. Sounds so good in my head, sounds so clear. Let's just forget him for now and enjoy the weekend. Both my girls are coming over for a movie night tomorrow; we don't get to do it very often, so it will be a welcome break.

CHAPTER FOUR

Once home, I eat some instant noodles and grab a drink. I put the music on and Heart sings 'All I Wanna Do is Make Love to You'. I shake my head and smile. I take myself off for a cool shower. Why does every song remind me of him? God, I need to get a grip – I've only known him for two weeks!

By eleven o'clock I'm feeling drunk, so I climb into bed and tell myself I really need to try and eat more, as that small pot noodle was not filling; but my stomach hurts and my brain hurts. The room is spinning, but I drift into a restless sleep of sexy toned bodies and the smell of Joop, his hands all over me, and those blue eyes. I dream about me kissing him and running my hand down his spine as he moves his toned torso on top of my sweat-soaked body; the way he rotates his hips, pushing me deeper into oblivion, kissing me with those beautiful lips; the smell of his skin, the look of lust in his eyes as he kisses my neck and nibbles my ear lobe, pulling on my nipples with his teeth, feeling him move faster and faster, rotating around and around, deeper and deeper, his solid manhood thrusting hard inside my swollen hole, until he trembles in my arms and he becomes completely undone, with sweat dripping down his face and him kissing me again softly; and, oh my god, his tongue moving down to my delicate area, and I think I'm going to come, just as I wake and the room becomes still and, oh my Lord, that was a vivid dream – it felt very real.

I try to catch my breath, staring at the ceiling. I can't help but wish it had been real and how I don't want to wake up; but thankfully sleep soon envelops me again and I don't wake up any more till morning, refreshed, but a little more frustrated. I try to eat my breakfast, but the thought of him just won't go away. Maybe I should look for another job? I don't think I can work near him knowing how sexy he is. Definitely not, I scream. Maybe I should just tell him that this isn't going to happen under any circumstances and that we should just keep it professional; maybe this is all in my head and maybe he is just being friendly. 'Yeah, Ruby, have you ever thought about that?' my inner demon scolds me. 'Yeah, because all bosses do that, right; all bosses corner their staff and make them feel like a fucking hot mess of emotions.'

I clear my bowl of fruit and nut and grab my phone. I'm so excited to see my girls today, I text them to find out what time they will be over and what snacks I should buy, and I instantly get a message back from Jessica, saying, 'Sorry, mum, change of plans.' Oh, damn, really? My heart sinks. She tells me her and a friend were going speed dating because it's only on once a month and this could be her month to find love; and I'm slightly disappointed, because I really don't want to be on my own – maybe I should go with them? But then I think, no, she wouldn't want her old mum there, so I don't let on how I feel, and I tell her to have an amazing time and be careful and that I love her. I get the same message from Belle ten minutes later, saying sorry, she was going clubbing with a friend who had just broken up with her boyfriend of four years. I tell her he was a cheating scumbag anyway and she didn't disagree. Again I tell her to be careful and have fun and that I love her lots and that Sunday roast will be at the normal time, and don't forget to tell Jessica she's bringing desserts. She replies with a big floating heart and 'I love you too, mum.'

I put down my phone and stare out of the window, thinking 'Now I feel lonely.' It's like a sudden realisation that I am totally alone. The house is too quiet, just my clock ticking on the wall above the oven. I can't dwell on it: I need to keep busy. It's not the girls' fault they have lives, plus we will see each other tomorrow; so I say to myself, 'It's just me and a bottle of vodka or two,' and I warn myself I need to eat a decent meal – if not, I won't be able to cook tomorrow.

The rest of the day goes by slowly and I potter around the garden, pulling weeds from my pot plants, and I clean out the fridge, which is empty most of the time. I even clean behind the couch while my music is playing loudly in the background: Tina Turner's 'What's Love Got To Do With It?' keeping me moving. I love to dance while I clean. This must be the normal kind of stuff we do on the weekend.

Later, I cook myself a jacket potato for tea with some tuna salad, trying to stay healthy, even if the vodka is bad. I clean up after myself and settle on the sofa and drain my first glass of cold icy heaven, wishing I had topped up the shelf with a few more bottles, thinking it may be a long night; I have to say, the alcohol shelf is never normally empty, but I must have drunk a lot in the last week, because there stand two lonely bottles.

My phone gives me a notification, making me jump. It's a text message, but I don't want to look because it's the weekend, and I don't have anyone who would want to text me, unless it is an advert for some sale that's happening; but then I think it could be the girls in trouble, so I pick it up and instantly I see it's from Mr Hails, with the first words being, 'Sorry to disturb you.' Fuck! Fuck! Fuck! What the hell is he messaging me for on a Saturday night? However, I can't help but smile. Oh my god, is this my first ever sext message? I laugh. I'm suddenly upright and I need more vodka, so I open the message and down another glass. It reads, 'Good evening Ruby.' What? He never calls me that. Oh my god, he never calls me that! My heart is racing. It then says that I had done an amazing job yesterday and I had some really good ideas. Wow, I'm in shock: he thinks I have good ideas! Then he asks me how my weekend was going so far and if I was alone. Why is he asking if I'm alone? What the fuck? Why would he want to know that? Then he asks me what I am doing right now. First, I am thinking that I knew I'd done an amazing job, even though he put me in that situation, the sexy beast; and why would he want to know about my weekend and if I was alone? What's it got to do with him? Why is he messaging me at home on a Saturday evening? My head is spinning, and I keep asking myself the same questions over and over. Does he not have a life of parties and beautiful people? I'm really confused, so I down another glass. Do I reply? Yes. What do I say? Say, 'Thank you, Mr Hails, I'm glad you like my ideas, and yes, I'm alone, not that it's got anything to do with you. I happen to like my own company, and I can waste hours listening to music, plus I can sit here naked and nobody will ever know.' I smile. Yes, that will do; after all, I couldn't start with, 'Oh, I'm sitting here alone drinking vodka because I don't have a life or a man, and well, I'm sad.' I decide on the first message – yes, that's what I'll send. He will be smiling at the thought of me naked. I press send, and instantly regret it. Oh my god, why? Why did I send that? Shit! I've only been there two weeks and I'm telling him I'm naked. Oh god, now what? I need another glass of vodka! This is insane. Oh fuck, I need a new bottle! What you should have said, Ruby, is, 'By the way, I can't stop thinking of you fucking my brains out, and why won't you kiss me or touch me?' My hand shakes as I pour another glass. I need music, I need to dance, so I put on the Vamps's 'Can We Dance?'. I need to forget him; he needs to leave me alone.

I instantly get a reply. Shit, here we go. It reads, 'Please call me Simon, and I quite like the thought of you wasting my time naked.' Boom, and with that I'm floored. I have no words! I slump to the floor in my near drunken state. He wants me to call him by his first name, which I didn't even know was Simon, and he likes the thought of me naked. The insides of my body are doing flips, and I'm so excited and nervous all at the same time and I'm really moving now. Meat Loaf bellows out of the speaker, singing 'Bat Out of Hell' at the top of his lungs. Does this mean he likes me? He is playing a very seductive game of chase. 'No, Ruby, don't be silly. I mean, look at you. He's just being polite.' But, feeling brave, I send a reply, 'Well, okay, Simon, why do you ignore me at work, and why won't you kiss me and why do you play games with me?' Send. Oh shit, fuck, shit, balls! Oh my god, Ruby, what an idiot. I instantly regret it, but only in a drunken sort of way.

I'm standing, re-reading his message back, and thinking, like, 'Oh, okay, I can call you Simon, but you still want to play games at work and make me feel all hot and flustered, while you're cool and calm, not giving a shit kind of way, like you hold all the cards and I'll just play along.' Why, oh fucking why, did I send that last message? I can't believe I just sent that. You stupid idiot; why, oh why, did you send that? I speak these words over and over. How are you going to face him now, Ruby.

I sit and will him to reply. The vodka has kicked in big time and I feel like dancing some more, so I put the next song on and sing – if ever in doubt, dance your heart out. Whitney Houston's 'I Wanna Dance With Somebody' comes alive, and I'm moving round the living room – well, stumbling. I don't get a reply from him for the rest of the night, and this kind of pisses me off; but I knew I was drunk, so maybe it was for the best. I'm not sure why he didn't just say sorry, or see you Monday. This is all crazy and I feel like smashing my phone, then I want to ring him, then I want to quit. Bloody alcohol! And talking of alcohol, I'm all out.

I soon fall silent, lying on the sofa, and as I stop the music, my drunken mind spinning in all directions, I slowly fall asleep into a peaceful slumber, waking up at 2am to go upstairs to pee. Taking a glass of water with me, I finally fall into bed and sleep like a baby.

Sunday lunch is full of fun and laughter with my girls. I love their energy, even if I am feeling a bit delicate. They have heaps to tell me about their crazy night and the man that Jessica got matched with, and she says he looked like a creepy boys' locker room coach. We all laugh at this, and I, too, tell them about Simon, and what I sent him in my drunken state, and we all just laugh again and take the mick out of each other, saying we are all mad and we must be related. Belle had danced the night away with some drunk hanging on her hips, but she ended up snogging the bouncer. I give her a look of disgust, then we all giggle. I miss that closeness with them, but I understand they have lives, too. I just want them to be happy.

We end the day with hugs and 'I love you', before they both head home. After Saturday night's drunken antics, I sleep like a log, trying not to think of sexy Simon. How the hell will I face him? Will he even say anything?

CHAPTER FIVE

I wake early, feeling ready for the day, ready for a new Monday and ready for Simon. Oh god, will he say something about the text or will he totally ignore me? I get dressed and put on my best jeans with a soft pink t-shirt tucked in the front: I look casual but trendy.

When I arrive at work, everyone is happy and in good spirits. We discuss our weekends and talk about idle stuff. Mervin says he shagged Mile's mum, to which Miles sticks his middle finger up. No way do I tell them about Simon, or how drunk I got.

We are all super-excited to get started on the Runaway Lingerie project, and when I say we, I mean *they*, because I just sit behind a desk all day and answer the phone; but it's a job, and I really enjoy it, like I mean, I really enjoy it. Even if Simon wasn't in the picture, I would still enjoy it.

Simon is in his office and I can't wait to see him. Well, that's a lie. I don't want to see him ever – that's another lie – but as usual he is playing his game of not talking to me. I bloody hate that game! Clearly he knows I'm at work, as he can hear us chatting, and when I go in to see Cecile, he sees me through the blind and just stares at me. It's so exhausting, all this uncertainty.

It is around twelve thirty that the others head out for lunch, asking me if I want anything, to which I reply, "No, I'm not hungry, but thank you." I really couldn't face food at this moment in time; my stomach is in knots. I just need to know what's going to happen and if he will fire me, or will he ignore it? Maybe he will just use this as another part of his twisted game. Maybe it didn't send; maybe it's sitting as 'unread'. Yeah, that's what happened: he hasn't even seen it! 'Yes, Ruby, of course, you keep lying to yourself,' says my inner bitch; so when the phone rings, I'm not expecting it to be Simon. Shit, fuck, shit! I can't speak – my mouth won't move and words won't come out.

He calmly asks to see me in his office. Oh fuck, I'm fired, I'm definitely fired, and it's all the vodka's fault. "Yes, of course, Mr Hails, right away," I mumble, putting down the phone. I stand slowly, then pull up my jeans and straighten my t-shirt as if on auto-pilot. I then take a deep breath and walk to his office. Do I knock, or just walk in? I decide to knock and I hear him say 'enter' in his firm but gentle voice. I turn the handle and walk in, and there he is, sitting on the front of his desk with a very straight face and arms folded, resting on his very firm chest. He has the lightest blue shirt on with dark blue-looking trousers, and his legs are firm as he sits there all strong looking, and I can't help but look at his crotch – it's a habit, okay? I feel sick, and I shut the door with a bang and immediately apologise for slamming the door. He does not smile at all – shit, he's pissed. I mean, he really looks pissed. I walk towards him and I stand a few yards back; he doesn't move or speak, and I stay silent; we just look at each other for what seems an eternity.

Finally, I step forward and say, "I'm sorry for what I sent you. I was drunk and it was the vodka making me brave."

He holds up his hand as if to tell me to stop, so I shut up and stare at him.

"Do you own a skirt, Ms Frankton?"

Wait, what, wow! Okay, I wasn't expecting that, and I'm confused; my face must have said it all, because he just looks at me with no expression. I eventually reply, "No, Mr Hails, I don't, as I've never felt comfortable in one," considering I class myself as a chunky butt – but I don't say that, of course.

We look deep into each other's eyes and finally he grins. "Please call me Simon," he says, then adding, "Ms Frankton, I think you should buy yourself a skirt and show off those long legs of yours."

Wait, what did he just say? Did I hear that right? I'm jumping inside, thrilled he thinks I have nice legs; but why would he say that? "Okay," I reply, looking all lost, "I will try to find one this weekend."

He takes a deep breath, stands up and walks a few steps closer to me; we are now only inches apart and I can feel his body heat and smell that delicious aftershave. He places his hands in his pockets and smiles, while all the time not taking his eyes off me "I would prefer you get it sooner rather than later," he adds.

Wait, hang on, say what now? He just stands there, staring deep inside me like he knows all my darkest secrets and all my wildest fantasies. "Yes," I say, as I try and stand up taller, and with a strong voice. "Of course, yes, I can do that, but why the sudden urge for a skirt?" I say, because I'm not convinced it's my legs he wants to see.

But he starts to move away and I'm gutted. He sits back on the edge of his desk and tilts his head to one side, offering a breathtaking smile just for me. "Well, Ms Frankton, I want to see you in a skirt, and in today's market that should be enough."

I'm screaming in my own head, he used my line. Yes, you can see them; yes, you can have them over your shoulders as you plough your hard cock inside me! 'Ruby bloody Frankton,' shouts my inner slut, 'you whore!' But I know it's what I need right now. "Okay, I mean sure thing, Mr Hails, I mean Simon," I reply, "I'll sort that for YOU as soon as possible." Yes, Ruby, good girl, you will sort that for HIM. I take a deep breath and clasp my hands in front of me and ask if that will be all.

He smiles and replies, "Yes, Ms Frankton, that will be all."

I turn and walk out of the room, closing the door behind me, not looking back. This battle is over – but who won? I'm ready for round two: if he wants a skirt, he will get a damn skirt, even though I hate skirts.

My week so far has been dull as shit. I've not seen Mr Hails – I mean Simon – at all; why does he play this game? 'Because he can, Ruby,' says my disappointed self. I've not managed to get a skirt because I look ridiculous in all of them, and I feel and look like a whale; plus, I've eaten everything in my entire house out of stress because I can't find a damn skirt and I can't shake off the thought of why he wants me in one so badly; he's never ever mentioned my legs before, so why now? Why does he have to be so awkward? Why can't he just say what he means, and why didn't he say anything about the message I sent? Why didn't I mention the damn text, and why can't he just take me in his arms and declare his undying love for me? I laugh out loud. 'You silly woman,' says my inner stupidity, 'you need a good seeing to and like now; things are getting desperate.'

Friday comes all too soon and Cecile talks with me about the lingerie advert that the boys have nearly finished and it sounds amazing. She then goes on to tell me all about the new man in her life: turns out speed dating can work and does work for all ages. Cecile was telling me she met a man named Roy –

Roy the farmer – and he's very handsome and he's taking her to a fancy restaurant tonight for a romantic meal, and he will probably pick her up in his tractor, I chuckle. Thankfully, she chuckles with me. I really am trying to look and sound interested, but I can't help but think of my lonely weekend ahead and it's killing me not seeing Simon. Even if I had got myself a skirt, he wouldn't see the bloody thing. Maybe I can book myself into a spa or a motel somewhere and just tell everyone how fantastic my life is and that I'm not slowly dying of loneliness and alcohol poisoning? Yeah, that could work, but then I'd miss seeing my girls.

We finish our conversation and I look at the clock: well, that's it then, it's five o'clock and it's home time – what a waste of a week worrying about ifs and butts; that man is a headfuck.

I grab my keys and head for the door. Everyone else has already gone and I have not seen Celina all week. What does she bloody do? I poke my head around the door and stop. I can see Simon's shadow through the slats, and I want to go say hi and tell him I'm thinking of him, and that we should just have sex and get it over and done with; once we do it, then it will get easier, and at least then being near each other won't be so awkward – or maybe he doesn't want to have sex with me and it's all in my damn old head.

I just don't have the guts to go see him, so instead I walk to the main door and outside. I close the door behind me and get in my car, and for some reason unbeknown to me, I start to cry – like I mean cry, the type of tears that yell 'I'm going to make your make-up run down your face and you will look a mess' cry.

I drive home listening to Janet Rushmore's 'You Keep Me Hanging On', and I think of all the men I've known in my life and how I've never really been in control of any of them – even my own husband didn't want me. I need vodka and I need my girls, and I need a holiday and sleep all rolled into one.

I get home and Belle is already there, making some spaghetti, which is a lovely surprise and I can't help but cry even more when I see her, and I want to hug her so tight. She sees me and instantly asks, "What's going on?", while all the time hugging me. "Oh, mum, talk to me," she says.

I then explain how I feel a fool, and how Simon makes me feel, and I ask her if I'm being silly. I tell her all about the skirt and how lonely I am, and I just need to get away – I need a break from all the men that have ever shit on me, and in the same sentence I just wish I could find someone who'll love me for me.

We chat for some time and I calm down. We eat spaghetti and meatballs over a glass of vodka, while Belle drinks tea as she is driving – she's so sensible for her twenty-three years. She then helps me clear the dishes and we chat some more and I ask if she's seen Jessica today and she says, "Yes, she said for me to tell you she will call you later."

Suddenly, my phone pings and I can see it's a number I know all too well – it's Simon, and in the same moment, Belle announces she has to dash, which makes me sad to be on my own again. But as we say our goodbyes walking to the front door, she tells me she loves me and if I need her I should call. I tell her thank you and to drive safely. I shut the door, and just like that I'm alone again.

CHAPTER SIX

I decide to take a quick shower and put on my favourite nightie, which kind of makes me feel sexy as it's very short. I want to put on some music, so connecting my phone to the Bose speaker, I pick a song. Yes, I say, this is a perfect singalong song – 'Toy Soldiers' by Martika – and I pour myself another glass of vodka. I realise I drink far too much, but at this precise moment I don't care. I look to change the next song and I suddenly remember about the message on my phone; so, grabbing it, I open the text: 'Hello Ruby, how's the search for a skirt going?'

OH MY GOD, what the fuck? That's not a headfuck at all. I am so not prepared for this. I drink another glass of vodka and contemplate my answer. I'm pacing the room now; what do I say, what do I reply? And all the time I'm thinking why, why now? Why not ask me at work? "Okay, I know I got this," I say in a new excited voice. I send back: 'No Simon I have yet to buy one, and in any case you wouldn't see it even if I did wear one because you never come out of your damned office, and you never tell me what you want, and you didn't mention what I said in the first text I replied to.' I send it, smiling to myself, but my heart is racing, and it feels good. I need him to know how he makes me feel.

PING. Another message. I read it out loud: 'Well what are you wearing right now?'

Holy shit, that's hot! I can't help but smile, because I think I look damn good in my skimpy almost see-through nightie that is way too short – I love it. I down my glass of vodka and send a reply: 'Well Simon wouldn't you like to know, I could be totally naked dancing around my living room listening to heavy metal, I could be having sex with a hot guy for all you care.' Send. 'Whoop, whoop, you go girl, you keep him hanging on,' says the slutty voice in my head, which is starting to fog.

Instantly, I get a reply and I'm so excited I nearly fall over; I can't wait to read it, and I'm almost knocked off my feet again by what he sends back: 'Well it does not sound like heavy metal to me, Ms Frankton, and I definitely don't think you're naked, or having sex with a hot guy, and I think you should pour yourself another glass of vodka.'

Wait, what? I'm confused. He can see me? Is he outside listening? What, wait a minute! I run to the living room window, but don't see anyone there, and in that second there is a knock at my door, and I freeze. Shit, no, it can't be. I try and calm my nerves as I close the curtains and run around, trying not to scream. Oh fuck, what if it is him? What the hell do I do now? I try to clear things away that I don't want him to see, like empty bottles of Coke and a half-eaten packet of crisps, plus the many chocolate wrappers on my coffee table. I stop and stand still for a second, making sure I've not missed anything, then I walk to the door and pause. What will I say? What will he say? Look at me, half bloody naked! What is he doing here anyway? Oh for fuck's sake, Ruby, just open the damn door. I'm shaking and I count to three. I open the door just a few inches and I'm hit with that smell, that sweet aftershave that can make a girl go weak at the knees, and that sexy smile looking goddamn hot. He's wearing a black suit with a black tie and leaning on the doorframe in a James Bond kind of way. I just kind of stare at him.

"Well," he says, "can I come in?" His voice is calm and soft.

"Oh, yes, I'm sorry, yes, come in." I'm a mumbling mess, as he walks past me into the living room, as if studying his surroundings, and I shut the door and walk past him. I say awkwardly, "I will just go put some clothes on… I mean, I'll just go change."

As I turn to try and walk away, he speaks quite boldly and says, "No, don't do that, you look good."

I'm really embarrassed, and I ask him, "Why are you here?"

He puts his hands in his pockets and steps closer to me. "I thought I would answer some of your questions from the other night," he says, and he's smiling hard at me.

"Oh, I see." I swallow hard. "Well, which one would you like to answer first?" I say, all shy.

He steps closer again and I step back. "You will have to give me a recap," he says, smiling.

Fuck me, he's hot! "Well, how about the one where I like my own company?" I give a shy smile.

He steps closer again, I step back. "No, Ruby, try again," he replies.

"The one about me wasting time naked?" Now I'm feeling hot and flustered.

He smiles and steps closer to me; I step back and I'm up against the wall. "Try harder," he breathes.

He's so close to me. "Well, maybe the one about you not touching me or kissing me?" I look down at my bare legs and go crimson.

He comes forward for the last time. I tell him I need to cover up; I need to get away from his intense stare. "No, you don't," he replies. He's pressed against me, those lips only inches away, my breathing heavy. Looking deep into my eyes, he say, "So you want to know why I won't kiss you?" I nod very enthusiastically. "And you want to know why I won't touch you," he adds. Again I nod away excitedly, as he takes his hands out of his pockets and places them on my waist. "Touch you like this?" he asks, all fucking sexy and wanting.

I can't bear it any longer; the air changes and we lock lips and it's on. My hands are in his hair and he grabs my buttocks, pushing me hard against the wall, making me moan into his mouth. He tastes so good. He stops and looks me in the eyes: fuck, I want this man so bad! Our lips touch again for the second time and it's electric; it is gentle and controlled, but sexy as hell.

"Okay," I say, "wait, Simon. Please, stop." I'm trying to wiggle away from him, not because I want to, but because I need to. I'm backing away saying this isn't professional, but he's smiling and coming forward, and as I back into the kitchen, he's in front of me and I know I can't resist.

Before I even say another word, he has pushed me up against the wall and has pinned both my hands above my head. He has one knee between my legs and he's pushing on my delicate parts. My breasts are pushed against his chest, and he kisses me long and deep, with our tongues touching in a mad hot mess, and both of us breathing hard. He releases my hands and I grab his hair, as he lifts my nightie up over my head to expose my breasts, and he instinctively takes one of my nipples into his mouth. I drop my hands down to his belt, frantically trying to unbutton his trousers, and I succeed. He lets me unbutton his shirt; all the while he doesn't stop kissing me, and my god, he can kiss – his lips soft against mine, his tongue exploring the inside of my mouth. I open his shirt to reveal his beautiful smooth chest – he's quite tanned, he's toned, but not over-the-top toned, and yes, he has the sexiest tribal tattoo that goes from his shoulder down his arm on to the right side of his chest.

He moves his hands to my waist and slowly pulls down my thong; all the while I'm looking into his eyes. I feel nothing but lust for this man. He's on his knees in front of me and I'm in awe, as he moves my legs apart and slowly runs his tongue up the inside of my leg, and my hands are in his hair again, as he reaches my soft, moist, extremely sensitive skin and he plunges his tongue deep inside my wet folds. Oh god, I really didn't think it would be like this.

He rolls his tongue round and round my clit, and as I cry out in pleasure he knows he's got me; but he doesn't stop – he's on a mission. He grabs my buttocks, squeezing tight, while I'm pulling his hair, dragging him in. But before I can enjoy the ecstasy any longer, my body betrays me and I break out into one of the hardest orgasms I've ever had, moaning loudly, while he tastes every last drop and feels the end of my ever-shaking body.

I feel I can't stand any more: my legs are like jelly. He stands to meet my gaze and I kiss him in a new and crazed form. I need to feel him between my legs, I need to kiss his perfect body, I need to explore every inch of him. I kiss his neck and my tongue runs down to his very erect nipples and draws circles around them. I keep going down his beautiful smooth stomach and all the way down to his beautiful-looking bulge. He is watching my every move as I release him from his underwear, and he springs up at me, ready to be tasted. He is big and I'm leaping inside at the thought of this – and I'm secretly saying 'thank you' to the gods for bringing this man to my door. I take him in my mouth and I watch his face closely as he inhales a short sharp breath of shock as I move with care not to hurt him.

It's been so long since I've even been close to a man, let alone had one in my mouth. I don't want to scare him off. He has a sweet, salty taste, and he's watching my every move; I can see he's loving it, because his eyes have glazed over and all I can see is pleasure in his face. His head falls back and he gives a low growl. He gently rests a hand on the side of my head, but not pulling me or forcing in anyway. I'm moving with him as he grinds before me. He places his other hand on his cock and looks down at me. I can see him smile as he gently pulls me up towards his lips. I could kiss this man all night, and as he grabs both of my hips, he spins me around so I walk backwards and my legs hit against the kitchen table. He lays me back and pulls me so my buttocks are at the edge of the table, and all the time I can't help but silently beg him to fuck me. He spreads my legs and steps between them; he guides himself inside me and I gasp. He feels so good, filling every inch of me. He is gentle at first, but then he really starts to move and the pleasure is almost too much to take. I feel like this is my personal mission to make this man explode. I hold his arms as if I may fall; he is strong, holding my legs like they weigh nothing. I know he is lost in our synchronised rotating, our heavy breathing matching one another. He leans down and kisses me again, and this seems to make him more excited and more in need. I want him to last as long as possible – I want him all night, because in my head I'm thinking, 'What if this is it; what if it's just one time; what if it's a pity fuck because he knows I'm into him big time and he's using me?' Well, if that is the case, I'm going to enjoy this for as long as I possibly can.

He is so close; we are all arms and legs and hot bodies, which only makes me want him more. He takes my left breast in his hand and lowers his mouth around my nipple, and at that same time he rams into me with a new sense of need. I cry out in pleasure; this man is a machine, every stroke bringing me to a hazy point of no return. He moves back up to meet my kiss and I can tell he's close by the way he makes a low grumbling sound, his hands on my thighs, gripping hard, as he wrap my legs around him, feeling his beautiful tight buttocks against my calves.

I fear the table may break soon, but this sends him over the edge; he can't take it any more, and as he lowers his head to my chest, he lets out a long moan through gritted teeth. He slows down, but does not stop completely and I hold him tight like he might break. I drop my legs back down and he relaxes on top of me, my head screaming, 'Wow, this man is every inch the god I thought he was.'

His breathing slows and he stops shaking, after what seems like an age. We just lay there as our heads return from the sky, with me running my fingers through his soft hair. I can feel his heartbeat against mine, and when he finally looks up at me he just gives me that award-winning beautiful smile and it's at that very moment I realise I think I'm in love. 'Not lust, Ruby,' my inner goddess chants, 'but love!'

I have come to the conclusion that even if this is for one night, my god, I'm fucking happy; even if we don't ever do this again, I will be satisfied to just look at his beautiful face. I will struggle being near him and not being able to touch him, I'm not going to lie, and we will have to discuss this at some point, but for now I am happy.

He moves up onto his hands, resting them both sides of my face; and, leaning down, he kisses me softly on the lips and I give a small smile. I think he can see the look of 'what the fuck was that?' in my eyes, as he asks me if I am okay, and I reply, "Yes, I'm fine," although I don't think I am fine – I think I'm far from fine.

He must know that all is not well, because he pulls me closer so I am now sitting on the edge of my table. He wraps his arms around me and I feel safe and wanted, so I pull him in tight, as if he's leaving and I'm never going to see him again. He smells so good: that after-sex smell mixed with Joop.

Foreigner's 'I've Been Waiting For a Girl' plays

on in the other room, and he looks up at me and says, "How about we get off this kitchen table and have a drink?" He kisses me again and again in short sharp bursts.

I smile and nod as we stand, my body aching from the cold table; suddenly, I feel all shy, as I'm looking for my nightie. I feel the need to cover up my body – he can't see all of this. I mean, yeah, before was okay, because we were in the moment, and I still had a hint of alcohol running through my veins; but now I need to hide it all. I find the nightie in a heap and I pull it on, along with my thong; all the while he just stands there, all Thor-like, with his cock swinging free. I can tell he is totally comfortable with his body and I envy him for it. He grabs his shirt and swings it over his shoulders, then picks up his trousers.

"I will be right back," I say, but as I try to leave the room, he stops me and pulls me close again.

"Are you sure you're okay?" he says, as he plants a small soft kiss on my lips. "You're awfully quiet," he continues.

I kiss him back with a desperate need to feel close to him, and he matches my tongue's rhythm as we get lost in the moment – a moment I don't ever want to end. My hands are fisting his hair, and with our heavy breathing slowing, he lets me pull away and I'm looking into those electric blue eyes. God, this man is beautiful!

"I just need to freshen up," I say, and as I head

for the door, I turn and look back at this god-like man still standing half-naked in my kitchen, and I smile, my inner slut dancing and chanting, 'We just got laid, girl; you just had dirty sex!' And with that, I dash upstairs to clean myself up and change into something more comfortable. That's the only thing with on-the-spot sex: you're not prepared for it, and you have to deal with the mess afterwards. I hope and pray that he's not left and we can maybe talk a little; I need to know why he just felt the need to turn up tonight.

As I walk back down the stairs to see him standing fully dressed in my living room, I feel ever so sad that he's put all of his clothes on and it implies he's leaving. 'Damn right he's leaving,' shouts my inner bitch; 'he got what he came for and you just let him have it.' I shake the thought from my mind because I know she's right: I made that way too easy, and as I walk over to him he holds out a glass of vodka for me. I take it and say thank you in a small child-like voice, not really sure how I should react around him now.

"Are you not having a drink with me?" I ask.

He looks at me in a sheepish way and clears his throat. "No, sorry, I have to go. I should have been at a charity function over an hour ago and my mother will probably have some choice words when she sees me."

"Oh," I say, "sorry if I've kept you from something," I say, looking into my glass.

"No, Ruby, it's not your fault at all," he says, as he comes close and puts his hands on either side of my face. He kisses me softly and looks straight into my eyes, saying, "I'm sorry, but I do have to go."

I step back and say, "It's fine, you go" – but in my head I'm screaming for him to stay.

He hesitates as if in limbo, then heads for the door and I follow like a lost puppy. He stops and turns back at me and says, "Enjoy the rest of your evening, Ruby," and he gives me that beautiful smile; and with that, he opens the door, walks out into the street and disappears.

I close the door, put my back against it and sink to the floor. What the hell just happened? I can't think straight. I feel used, I feel like he just used me. I can't stand it any longer, so I get up, turn off the music and I go up to my bed. I need to sleep and forget about this night, but the smell of him is still on me and I can feel him between my legs, I can still feel his kiss, and I want him back here now, I want him to stay with me and hold me; I feel empty.

I fall asleep and stay asleep like I've not slept in years. I don't think I moved from the same position all night.

CHAPTER SEVEN

Saturday morning comes all bright through my window, as I forgot to close the curtains. I drag myself to the shower to wake myself up. Did last night actually happen, I ask myself. Was I dreaming the whole thing? Then I feel the ache between my legs and I know it was real. I've not had sex like that for years, not even with my ex-husband – who, by the way, is one boring son-of-a-bitch and I don't know why I stayed with him so long; it was probably for the girls' sake, or the security, who knows? I dry my hair and dress: it's a sweat pants kind of day. I brush my teeth and head downstairs.

My phone lays dead next to the stereo and the smell of Joop and sex lingers in the air. I open the window to try to get rid of the smell – I don't want the girls to know what I did, although I will need to tell someone at some point; it's what us women do. Once I've recharged my phone, I have five missed calls from Jessica and three messages from Belle asking if I'm okay, and why won't I answer my phone? So I reply 'Sorry I'm fine and I just went to bed and forgot to charge it.' Then I phone Jessica back, telling her my phone died and I left it downstairs and that I'm fine and to stop worrying. They both seem happy and they say to see me tomorrow.

I pop into town with a new sense of urgency for a skirt, and I finally find one in one of the high street stores: it's black and just above the knee, and I feel quite sexy in it, I must admit. I just hope Simon likes it; that's if he will even get to see it.

Sunday flies by too quickly. Me and the girls have a good giggle, although I think they can tell I'm holding something back, but neither one presses me for an answer. Sunday night is quiet, too, and I wonder what Simon might be doing, and why I haven't got a message from him asking me if I'm okay. This kind of pisses me off, but I can't think too much as it will tear me up inside; maybe I should text him. No, don't be silly, Ruby! I scold myself for thinking such a stupid thing. I decide to have an early night, and I will ask him tomorrow what the fucking deal is – I need some answers.

Monday morning and I'm ready to go: got my new skirt on, with a creamy floral blouse, and my new black boots. I feel fucking good, I say to myself when I walk past the mirror in the hall. I have a new thong on and my hair is up in a high ponytail.

Leaving the house, I lock the door and climb into my car. Once I start her and turn on the radio, Roxette's 'Listen to Your Heart' bellows out and I can't help but wonder why all the songs I hear are related to Simon and love; it's kind of pissing me off.

The morning is cool; it rained last night, so the air smells clean and fresh. Pulling up at work, I can see Simon is already here – of course he is – and just as I exit my car, I get a very chirpy 'good morning' from Celina.

"You look fabulous today, Ruby," she says. She looks amazing as usual in a tight-fitting navy blue dress and killer heels, and I see Cecile pulling into the car park all slow and careful. We walk in together, having a chit-chat about general shit – we talk about Celina's diet and how she can only eat certain foods. I really couldn't care less. I sound awful and I don't mean to be, but my head is a mess, so the whole time I just smile and nod in the right places.

Miles and Mervin are laughing as they walk in, so at least someone's in for a good day. I can hear Mervin say something about leaving Miles's mum in bed this morning – Miles, of course, has a few choice words to say about that – and we all settle at our desks after grabbing coffee and tea. I fire up the pc and wait for the screen to load. I even say good morning to my cactus and can't believe it's still alive. Celina walks straight into Simon's office and I'm so envious that she can just do that. She's in there for a good hour or more, and when she leaves his office I see his door is left open and she pops her head round the doorway and says, "Mr Hails would like a word when you're free."

Oh, great, I think, here we go; but I decide not to

go in straight away. I think, 'No, make him wait, Ruby; he can damn well wait for me and see how he likes being ignored.'

Another hour passes, and everyone gets up and heads out to get lunch. Celina has been gone for ages, so this is my perfect moment to go and see what he wants. I need answers. I'm feeling confident, and I love my new skirt and the way it makes me feel. I head to the door and peek around the corner; he looks up from his computer and gives me that beautiful smile.

"Come in, Ruby, and shut the door, please." He seems happy, so I do as I'm told and quietly close the door; but I don't move – I'm rooted to the spot. He walks over all sexy and confident, and stops in front of me with his hands in his pockets, his white shirt tucked into his black trousers and his sleeves rolled up to his elbows. He looks fucking hot! I look at him with dreamy eyes and instantly I want to kiss him, but I have a feeling it's not what he wants, so I calmly ask him if there is something he needs, and he smiles that award-winning smile and replies, "No, I just wanted to see you in that lovely skirt and look at those beautiful legs." He looks me up and down, and I sigh a long sigh; and, feeling brave, I touch his arm and he immediately stands back. Now that's a shocker. I feel stupid.

"Have I done something wrong?" I ask. "Maybe I should go," I say, stepping back.

"No," he replies, not taking his eyes off me, "I just can't do this at work." And there it is, there's the confirmation I needed – he wants me on his terms and under his conditions. Well, fuck that, and I instantly feel used.

I take an even bigger step back and look at him with anger in my eyes and my hands on my hips. "So it's okay for you to come to my home and fuck me on my kitchen table, but I can't come to your office and at least touch you or kiss you." I can see he's pissed. He pulls his hands from his pockets and takes a deep breath. "Well fuck that," I say, and as I turn to leave, he grabs me from behind. He is strong and he smells so good.

"Fine," he says through gritted teeth, "have it your way." He marches me over to his desk and flings me across it so I'm flat on my stomach.

"Simon!" I yell. I'm lying on paperwork and documents, but he doesn't care. He pulls up my skirt and yanks down my thong, spreading my legs with his foot, and with one swift move he undoes his trousers and fills my throbbing pussy with his long hard cock. I cry out in pain and pleasure, my hands grabbing the side of the desk for support. There's no stopping him, and he grabs my hips, ploughing into me. He is rough and fast and in desperate need to get this over with. I cry out and after a few more thrusts he begins to lose control, and before I can even begin to enjoy it, he reaches his climax with a grunt through gritted teeth and a loud "Fuck me, Ruby!" for good measure. He falls on top of me, but only for a second, before pulling out. I wince and slowly pull myself up. He hands me a tissue and asks that I don't make a mess. I can see his sneaky smile. I can't help but smile and think how classy. I snatch the tissue and put it between my legs, before pulling up my thong and pulling down my skirt. Once he's done his trousers back up and wiped the sweat from his brow, he moves closer to me. The air is super-charged, and I can't stand it any longer, so I lunge at him and kiss him with every ounce of my soul. He kisses me back just as hard, and we explore each other's mouths until we run out of breath.

I pull away and after a moment I ask him what the hell that was all about. He looks perplexed, like I've just given him some puzzle to solve. "I'm sorry, that was out of order," he replies; "but now you know why I wanted you to get a skirt so bad," he adds.

I smile and shake my head. "You have been planning this for two weeks," I say.

He nods and say, "Sorry."

"So what now?" I ask.

He looks deep into me and tilts his head. "Now, I really need to get back to work. I'm sorry."

Wait what? "So that's it?" I say. "Yet again you have your way and it's 'See you later, Ruby'?"

"Look," he says, all business like, "we are friends, yeah?"

I must look like a rabbit in the headlights, because all I can say is, "No, Simon, you're my fucking boss!" I'm so angry.

He genuinely looks sad as I stand in front of him with my arms folded. He sighs and speaks quietly. "The others will be back soon."

"Wow!" I say, placing my folded arms by my side with clenched fists, my face in a twisted mess. "Just wow, Simon." I turn and leave the room, slamming the door behind me. I can't face being near him at the minute; I'm so angry and confused all at the same time. He's just using me for his own pleasure, which in my head I know is not true, because I get a lot of pleasure from this beautiful man. I just don't understand why he can be so hot and then so cold towards me. Surely things like that don't happen in real life?

I walk to the toilet to clean myself up, and spend the rest of the day sitting quietly at my desk, the skirt making more sense now. I can't even be bothered to answer the damn phone, and the day just seems to go by with me sitting still and everyone around me in super-fast mode – in and out they go, grabbing coffee and using the bathroom, giving me a 'hey, Ruby, are you okay?' now and again.

I finally snap out of it and decide this weekend I'm going to get away: I need some time away from everything and everyone. I can't sit home alone again, and I can't chance him coming round, so I search up a local spa and make a booking. I may even leave my phone at home, I think to myself; but then a thought of the girls needing me comes into my mind. I'll explain to the girls later; they will be happy I'm getting away from it all, and this will be the best money I've spent in a long time.

Feeling more positive, I finish the rest of my day in peace. Celina breezes in and then straight back out. She's a strange one. Five o'clock comes around and I can't wait to leave. Shutting down my pc, I gather my things, and don't even say goodbye to the others. I just get in my car and drive away, back along the A47, with Passenger singing 'Let Her Go' ringing in my ears.

I feel wretched; I need a bath and a drink. Back in the safety of my own home, I drown myself in the tub and drink myself into a near coma. The rest of the night is a bit of a blur, but I do remember dancing and singing out loud to Celine Dion's 'All By Myself', feeling like Bridget Jones.

Tuesday morning I'm feeling a little delicate as I head into the office. There is no sign of Simon anywhere and that I find unusual. Celina walks in all breezy and makes herself a coffee and takes a seat on the small sofa just to the right of my desk. She kind of looks lost, and I ask her if everything is okay.

"Oh, yes," she replies, looking into her coffee and giving a sigh. "It's just when Simon takes himself off for a few days I feel at a loss as to what to do."

Takes himself off for a few days? What, why? And with a new breath in my lungs, I sit up straight and finally ask Celina what it is she actually does.

She turns to face me and gives a small giggle. "Well," she's says, "I'm basically Simon's confidant." She smiles. "Basically, I'm his right hand woman," and she gives another small giggle. "So, like, if he broke his arm," she continues, "I could step into his shoes and kind of nearly do what he does." I'm in awe of her: she's a very intelligent woman. "Oh," she says, all exited, putting down her coffee and leaning forward, "and I know his every move," she adds. She lowers her head as if looking over some imaginary glasses "I know all his dirty little secrets" – and I can't help but feel she's looking right inside me and she knows that Simon fucked me across his big oak desk.

I smile and say, "It seems like a really demanding job, being at his beck and call. Not that I would mind," I add. "I mean, look at him!" I laugh.

She then lowers her voice to a whisper and leans forward again, saying, "Honestly, Ruby, some of the things he does and the deals he makes would have you disgusted." She sits back up and grabs her coffee; and with that, I'm presuming she means all the women he's had and all the shady deals he's done to get to where he is – but am I just being bitter over what happened yesterday?

We don't talk any more as her phone rings and

she walks off into the other room to answer it. My heart starts to hurt, and I think, 'Am I just another notch on his bed post?' I need to know more, but I'm scared of the answer. 'He's bad news, Ruby,' says my inner sensible self. 'You need to be careful.'

CHAPTER EIGHT

The rest of the week has come and gone, and there's been a rain cloud hanging over my head ever since my chat with Celina. I miss him, I really do; I miss knowing that he's in the next room, that he's only a few short feet away.

Getting in my car, I call my girls to let them know I'm heading off to the hotel and that I love them. It's five thirty and I need to get a move on if I'm to enjoy the rest of the evening in peace. I'm just glad I packed my small case this morning, saving me a lot of time.

The girls tell me to have a super weekend and to relax, and they even joke, telling me I might meet the man of my dreams in the hot tub. I laugh and say, "Yeah, right, things like that don't happen to people like me." We say our goodbyes and I leave the car park. I turn on the radio and yet another song that reminds me of Simon fills my ears: Paul Young sings 'Every Time You Go Away', and I can't help but sing along and think of where he might be.

After an hour's drive, I arrive at the Sun Valley hotel and spa, and it looks beautiful from the outside – very grand looking, all lit up in the dark, so you know exactly where to go, like something out of a

Hollywood movie, all fresh-cut grass and colourful raised flower beds, and a beautiful water feature in the middle of the gravel driveway. I park my car at the main reception and take my small case inside. I think I may have overpacked, but the only thing on my mind now is having a drink at the bar. God, let there be a bar, I laugh.

I am instantly greeted with a very energetic "Good evening, madam," from a man standing at reception. "How may I help you this evening?" he adds.

Wow, what an entrance: beautiful old vases filled with freshly cut roses sit on huge concrete pedestals; there is a giant chandelier that hangs from the ceiling in the middle of the room, all lit up and grand; a long shiny gold desk to my left; and a double glass door to my right, which is open and I can see the bar and I smile; and to the left of the glass doors there is one of two elevators with shiny gold doors that you can see your face in.

I can't help but match this man's enthusiasm with my own. "Good evening," I reply, "my name is Ruby Frankton and I'm here to check in."

He smiles and I see his name tag reads 'Thomas' with 'Supervisor' underneath, and he gently taps on a keyboard while asking me if I've had a wonderful day and he hopes my journey was not too long. He looks late thirties and has blond hair combed neatly over to one side. He has a very well maintained goatee, and lovely hazel eyes that seem to sparkle when he talks. He is slim and tall, and I can tell he loves his job. I can see he wears his black, neatly pressed trousers and his super-neatly pressed white shirt with pride, and a bright red tie hangs from his neck. He must spend ages getting that perfect, and this alone makes me smile. He hands me a plastic door key and tells me that I'm on the third floor, room Sixty Nine. Oh, how appropriate, I think to myself. I try to hide my smile with my hand.

"Well, I wish you a pleasant stay," he says, as he comes around the desk, asking me if I need help with my bags.

I say, "No, thank you, I'm good."

He smiles and says, "If you're sure, Ms Frankton." He holds out his hand to show me to the elevator, and he even presses the button for me. He hums as we wait, then I thank him and walk inside. As the doors close so that I am now alone, I chuckle and shake my head. I press the button marked Three and the lift rises but doesn't make a sound. With a ping the speaker announces my floor and the doors open to a brightly lit corridor and a smell of fresh flowers fills my nose. A perfectly vacuumed navy blue carpet covers the floor, and I see fresh magnolia walls and a small gold plaque with arrows telling which rooms are in what direction: my room is to the right, and I only have to walk a few feet and I'm at my door. Even the doors are a shiny gold metal, with a big Sixty Nine right above the spy hole.

I can't help but smile as I swipe the key card in the door and the light turns green. I enter and turn on the light, the door closing behind me. I'm greeted with a king-size bed and a swan-shaped towel folded neatly at the end and a red rose tucked into his towel wing. To my right is a small bathroom with a lovely glass shower; there is a desk opposite the bed with a small kettle and two cups, and an assortment of teas and coffee beside it, and a phone to call reception. It's got extra big buttons and is bright red to match the blinds and the bedspread. I throw the key onto the desk, above which is a huge flat screen tv, and I think, 'Great, I've paid all this money to come to another bedroom in another building forty minutes from my own home to watch tv.'

I put down my case at the end of the bed and walk to the window; the view is breathtaking, with rolling fields and freshly cut lawns and huge concrete statues of naked men showing off their small dicks, and I chuckle at the sight of them. The moon has just come out, which makes the scenery all the more pretty. Below me seems to be a decked area and I can see benches and large umbrellas and what looks like people drinking, and I immediately think that's where I need to be; I need a drink.

I can't even be bothered to unpack my case. I just grab the door key from off the desk and head downstairs, back into the lobby and past the still smiling Thomas to the bar, which is just across from reception. It's large and clean and has more huge vases of flowers dotted everywhere. I'm guessing vases are the theme here. Lots of tables, small and big, fill the room, all with pristine white tablecloths and super sparkling wine glasses turned upside down. There is a long shiny bar to the left, with a gold rail running all the way along, and navy blue and gold bar stools to sit on. I head in that direction and wait my turn. I'm soon served a very tall double vodka and Coke by a very pretty, slim-looking lady, her hair neatly wrapped in a bun almost sitting on top of her perfect head. She, too, is in black trousers and a crisp white shirt; her name is Michelle and she, like Thomas, is all smiling and in my eyes far too happy for a job like this, so I pay her and say thank you, while she says, "You're welcome."

Turning, I decide to head outside to the cool night air, and sit at one of the benches. Four other guests are chatting at the table next to me. It's warm out, and I'm glad I'm wearing my lightweight jeans and a pale pink off-the-shoulder sweater over a black kami. I take out my phone and see I have no messages and no calls; typical daily life of Ruby Frankton, I scoff.

I order some food from the bar and I sit, quietly picking through my chicken salad, I come to the conclusion I just need to get drunk, so I head to the bar and order another vodka, feeling sorry for myself; and as the pretty lady hands it over, I try to give her some cash, but she shakes her head and says, "No charge." I look at her all puzzled and she smiles at me, while pointing her finger to the right of the bar, saying, "That gentleman at the end of the bar already paid."

I swing round to my left and there stands Simon, looking fucking hot in his shiny silver suit and that killer smile, and I almost drop my drink. I can't quite believe what I'm seeing – he's here! We just stand and stare at each other from across the room, neither one of us speaking. Michelle has already retreated back to whatever she was doing, and after an age he walks over and stands inches away from me. I can smell that succulent aroma of his aftershave and I'm transported to my kitchen table and his big oak desk where he so savagely seduced me. He holds up his hand for Michelle and orders himself a whisky on the rocks, and I can't help but think he didn't strike me as a whisky drinker. Michelle places the drink on the bar in front of him and he slides her some cash. He sips slowly with those perfect lips of his, and I can't help but think what the fuck is he doing here and how the hell did he know I was here? I'm stunned and I can't say anything except, "What the fuck?"

He looks sheepishly at me and says, "I knew you would be here because all company computers are monitored." I blink wildly as he continues, "And I saw your reservation and well, I had to see you."

I shake my head in utter shock. "So first you want

me, then you don't, and now here you are yet again invading my personal space. Well, I'm sorry, Simon, but this," I say, shaking my finger between us, "is not happening." I down my drink then slam the glass on the bar, turning to walk away. I hear him put down his glass and I know he's right behind me; in one sense I'm glad he's here, but in another I think, 'You goddamn stalker, how fucking dare you! Can I not just have some me time away from you and your beautiful face?'

I continue through the lobby to the elevator and he's right behind me. I press the button and wait; he's standing behind me with his hands in his pockets – I can see him in the shiny elevator. I can't wait much longer, but I stand there, tapping my foot, and all the while he says nothing, standing there like a cat waiting to pounce; so I turn and head for the stairwell just right of the reception desk. I push open the door and it slams against the wall hard, and I make for the stairs. He swings the door open and he's right behind me, and I practically sprint up the first flight in the hope he won't keep up; but I am wrong, because he makes it look way too easy. But I keep going, yelling at him to please stop following me.

I'm on the second flight when suddenly he grabs me from behind and he swings me around and pushes me hard up against the concrete wall, his mouth on mine in a frenzy of need and want, his body pushing me back, not letting me move. I kiss him back, because I can't resist, but then I push him away; we stare at one another with our breathing out of control, my face telling him I'm mad. Again I break free from his clutch and head for the next flight of stairs, but he's too quick and he catches me again and in one swift movement I am falling backwards, lying on the stairs with the soft carpet behind my back, and he is on top of me, pinning me down. I try my hardest to push him off; we are both struggling and grunting, out of breath.

"Simon, no!" I snap, but he tries hard to undo the zip on my jeans and yank them down, while I desperately try to stop him. My shoes are off and so are my jeans, as he pushes me back down and yanks my thong so hard with his free hand it rips right off. I'm in desperate need to get away from him; this just can't happen, not now, not here – for fuck's sake, it's a hotel! Before I can move any more, his head is between my legs. I'm trying to wiggle and squirm to escape, and I cry out in frustration. I hit his shoulders with closed fists and yank at his hair, but his mouth is on me, licking my hard clit around and around. I try to push his head away and climb backwards up the stairs, but his grip on my waist is too strong; he is relentless as he moves with me, and I'm losing the fight against him. I'm getting lost in the pleasure and I can feel myself on the brink of coming, until he slides his middle finger deep inside me and I explode. I succumb to his tongue, my orgasm taking me away from reality, and I swear I can see stars. My shaking body comes to a still silence, and he looks up at me with wild eyes. I can't move, and with one hand he unbuttons his trousers; he is quick, like he has a need to be filled, and in a split second he is deep inside me with a new sense of greed, pushing me harder onto the stairs. I cling to his strong shoulders, crying out in pleasure and pain. He feels so good; my body aches, and I'm hurting from the stairs in my back, but I don't care. After a few hard thrusts and some very loud moans and me trying not to cry out, he finally lets go, filling me with his salty mess, and he collapses with a low grumble and a gasping breath on top of me. He is done, and so am I. He has got me right where he wants me.

Catching our breath, we look at each other and I can't help but laugh. "What have you done to me, Ruby Frankton?" he says with heat in his eyes.

All I can do is smile back and say, "You got me good, Mr Hails." I am completely and utterly in love with this beautiful man that lies over me, with his cock still pulsing deep inside me. There is nowhere else I want to be right now, but after a few minutes I start to move, as I know someone could walk into the stairwell at any moment and they would not want to see all of this. I say out loud, "This is one of the hottest things I've ever done in my life."

He smiles and pulls me to my feet, holding me steady. I scramble to put my jeans back on, while he straightens his shirt and tucks it back in his trousers, then see my thong ripped apart on the floor. I'm so embarrassed, as he looks at me and looks at the floor, and with a hunch of his shoulders, says in a cheeky voice, "Whoops, sorry!"

I laugh again and pick them up off the floor and put them in my pocket. I feel all yuk and sticky between my legs as I put my shoes back on, and I can't stop thinking how sexy it all is and how quick it all escalated. "I need to take a shower," I tell him with a hint of sadness in my voice, because he will probably leave now; he's had his fill, and clearly that's why he came, but I don't want him to go. I want him to stay and hold me in his arms.

He comes close and he places his hands either side of my head and says in a slow, sexy way, "I'm sorry I can't stay with you."

Wait, what? "Wow!" I say, all surprised, but I don't know why I'm surprised, because this is what he does best. "I'm used to it now," I say with a look of disgust on my face.

He steps back and looks at me as if to say you don't understand. "We are just friends, yeah?" he says with a smile.

I smile when he says it. "Yes, and you're my boss." God, this man is hot! I look to the floor, because I need to cry. "You need to leave," I say. "I need to shower and freshen up."

He steps closer and kisses me softly. I let him,

because I still want him so badly. "I'm sorry, Ruby,"
he says all apologetic, and with that he takes my hand,
puts it to his mouth and kisses it gently, then turns and
walks back down the stairs out of sight.

I am alone once more and it hurts. Once I'm on
the third floor, I walk silently until I reach my door,
and I can't contain my emotions any more – I want to
shout it out and tell the world I'm in love with a man
who can't commit.

CHAPTER NINE

I enter the room and turn on the light. I walk over to the bed and sit, taking off my shoes. Again, I shake my head, then head straight for the shower. I need to get out of these jeans. I strip naked and turn on the shower and as I step in under the cool water, I can feel the evening's tension slip away from my body. I touch myself between my legs and it's a reminder of Simon being there only moments ago. I feel him inside me, his skin against my skin, his kiss, his tongue exploring my mouth, his soft lips against mine, the cool running water splashing over my shoulders and down my breasts, the way he grabs my buttocks, the way he squeezes with an intense grip. I reach my hands around to my front and gently cup my beasts, rolling my nipples between my fingers, caressing my sensitive skin. I feel an all too familiar aching between my legs and I need him inside me. This man is my god. I put my fingers inside my swollen vagina and start to rub my clit in long, soft strokes. I am in complete control of my body and I do not stop rubbing and stroking over and over, thinking of Simon. I feel his hands, I taste his kiss, I smell his skin; my body builds to an exploding point of pleasure and I give a low muffled groan and I come quietly, hardly making a sound. I'm done; my body slows from my trembling orgasm, I lean on the wall and feel lost from wanting him so badly.

I finish cleaning myself and I wash my hair. I turn off the shower and climb out, grabbing a towel, and head back into the bedroom. I pick up the phone to call reception and order one large vodka and Coke. I'm sitting on the end of the bed and holding a swan made from a towel, and I can't help but think it's fascinating and how do they get it so perfect? I'm on auto-pilot, the memory of the stairwell fading away, so I lie back on the bed, looking at the ceiling, and think, 'Why did I let him do that? Why did I let him walk away? What's he's not telling me?'

Just then, there is a knock at the door, so I jump up to answer it, but not before wrapping the tiny towel tighter around my waist. Thank god it's a woman bringing the drinks when I look through the peep hole; I think, any man coming to the door and seeing me in this tiny towel may have dropped the drinks on the floor. I say thank you, and go back to sitting on the bed. I down my drink in one; it's really cold, and I don't know if I've lost the plot or I'm really thirsty, and with a shake of my head as the cool liquid slides down my throat, I put the glass down and giggle – like I mean lost-it giggle. I feel like a naughty teenager.

I whip off my towel, revealing my very naked body. If only he were here to see it! I lie down again, feeling dizzy and tired, like dog-tired, and grab the phone to order another large vodka and Coke. "I may as well get plastered, Ms Frankton," I say out loud, shaking my head, and I give the biggest smile: I love it when he says my name like that.

The drink is very welcome when it arrives – all this sex in stairwells is thirsty work, I think to myself. I want to call my girls, who are amazing, by the way; Belle is a student nurse at the local hospital and Jessica is a very talented writer – she writes for the local newspaper. They live in a shared house with Jessica's friend Jamie, who is a talented make-up artist, but who is messy and dysfunctional. They have both done well for themselves.

Eventually, I fall asleep, and dream of me and Simon sipping cocktails on a deserted beach and him telling me he loved me. When I wake up a few hours later, my head hurts and I can't help but think, 'Why do I let him keep doing this to me?' "What a jerk!" I say out loud, and my heart sinks. I reach for my phone out of my bag and call the girls: I need to hear a friendly voice. We chat while I make a cup of tea using the small jug on the desk. Thank god for my girls, because I would have absolutely no-one. We chat for some time and they ask if I'm having a relaxing time and if there are any hunky guys here. I laugh and say, "Well, considering I only arrived last night, absolutely not!"

After telling them I love them and that I will see

them soon, I think about going for a swim, and we hang up the phone. I still check my phone for a text in case he, by some slim chance, has sent me one saying sorry. I open my suitcase and pull out my bathing suit: it's blue with tiny white flowers all over it – and now I've got it on, I feel and look really old; it's tight on my skin and maybe I will buy a new one, but I need to swim and wash the night away. I put my clean jeans over the top, tie up my hair, which is getting far too long, slip on my pink hoody and grab my bag, before heading downstairs to the pool, which is just right of the elevator, down a long hallway at the back of the bar.

I pass a kind-looking cleaner coming out of the ladies' toilets, pushing a cleaning cart in front of her. She looks at me and smiles, so I smile back and say hello. On the wall just above her head is a sign saying 'Pool this way', so I know I am going in the right direction. The pool area is lovely; the pool is large and square, with a jacuzzi added on to the end, which overlooks the gardens. There are blue and white striped sun loungers dotted all around the poolside, so I place my bag on one that's empty and I undress.

Climbing into the pool with the water all around me is fantastic; it makes me feel super-relaxed. I float for a while and swim for about an hour. I really am unfit, because two laps in and I'm ready to have a heart attack. Climbing out of the pool and sliding into the jacuzzi, I think to myself this is heaven, with the hot water and the bubbles making me sleepy. It's really relaxing, and I wish I had room for one at home. I can feel my skin starting to shrivel, but having a spa all to myself in this beautiful hotel is a rare thing for me, so I stay here for a while longer. I nearly fall asleep, it's so peaceful, but finally I decide to get out and head back up to my room, using the changing room to get dressed. I can see myself coming here again, and especially if he's going to turn up and surprise me. I can't help but think of him, like he's on my mind all the time. I am angry with him, yet I still want him.

As I enter my room, I see my bed and fall onto it, the memories of last night bouncing around my head, and it makes me smile. I drift off to sleep – I'm so tired it's unreal – and when I wake a couple of hours later, I'm still in the same position. As I roll over and stare at the ceiling, I think to myself, 'He is a headfuck, he really is. He's more complicated than a woman, and it's driving me insane. He can be so cold and yet so fucking hot. Like, seriously, I've not heard from him all day.' I contemplate sending him a text, but then I think he may not like that; maybe I should just call and see if he's busy – but again he may not like it. Oh, what am I going to do? I sigh. I know, I'll shower and shave and make myself look beautiful. Yes, this will cheer me up; at the end of the day, what else have I got to do?

The shower is cool on my skin and as it runs off

my breasts I think of him and his hand touching me between my legs. I could cry. I hate feeling this way; it sucks to be Ruby right now. But in just over two hours, I'm finally ready and looking hot. 'Ha, who am I kidding?' I think to myself: it's just skinny jeans and casual white t-shirt and my new black boots.

Grabbing my lightweight jacket from the closet, I head downstairs for a nice filling meal; and maybe, you never know, he will appear again just like last night. My god, he is a beautiful man. I touch my lips at the thought of his soft kiss. Fuck, I miss him.

I pick up the door key and head down to the bar. For the first time in a long time, I'm hungry, so when my grilled chicken breast on a bed of creamy mash with a sweet chilli sauce arrives, I tuck in, and it's delicious. I've not eaten properly since Wednesday. I sit and watch the world go by and I can't help but wonder where I would be if I had not taken this job, or they had not hired me, and why didn't he stay? Why won't he stay? It has really bugged me, and the more I think of it, the more it hurts my heart.

A few drinks later and I head up to my room for a fun-filled night of tv and sleep, alone. I'm feeling pretty tired now, anyway, I must admit. Once I'm back at my room, door number Sixty Nine – I still can't get over that number, I giggle – I dress in my comfy sweats and I order a few more drinks from reception. I wish I had some music to listen to: I should have brought my pods. Turning on the tv, I have a limited number of channels to watch, so I turn it off again. I down my last drink and pick up my phone, looking blankly at the screen; no messages, no calls, nothing. Nobody loves me, I think, so I decide to climb into my bed and it takes me all of two minutes to fall asleep, tossing and turning and dreaming of naked bodies and sexy blue eyes.

Sunday morning comes and goes. I have some breakfast and go for a swim. I then take a long walk around the grounds, which truly are beautiful, and the smell of fresh-cut grass is one of my favourites. I head back in and up to my room to pack my case, before going to reception to check out. Thomas is still there, smiling more than ever, and I think to myself why is he so fucking happy? Jesus, Ruby, I say, snapping at myself, he's allowed to smile – not everyone is old and cranky like you.

Thomas looks up at me and in a very chirpy voice asks, "So, how was your stay, Ms Frankton? Was everything to your satisfaction?"

As I hand him the door key, I reply in a defeated kind of voice, "It was lovely, thank you. I've had a wicked time" – and when I say wicked, I think of the stairwell and how the cleaner will have some juicy residue to clean off the carpet! I still can't believe I did that.

"Well," Thomas pipes up, "we do hope to see you here again soon."

I tell him that I have a room service bill I need to

settle and he looks at me quizzically. He taps again on the keyboard and looks up at me. "Nope, Ms Frankton, it's all paid up," and he smiles again.

"Wait, what?" I say. "How? I haven't paid it," I continue, my mind in overdrive.

He smiles again and says, "Well, it looks like you have a fairy godmother."

I look up to the grand chandelier and give a big sigh. 'Simon, you little shit!' shouts my brain, and I can't help but smile. "Well, thank you," I say to Thomas as we say our goodbyes.

I head to the car park to my car. You wait till I see Simon on Monday – he's going to get a piece of my mind! Sounds great when I say it in my head, but actually being face to face with him is something different altogether.

The drive home is boring and quiet. I don't even turn on the radio; I just listen to the sound of my car and the thoughts in my head. I message the girls and tell them I'm home safely.

CHAPTER TEN

Monday morning and I'm up early. I've eaten and I feel sexy in my black skinny jeans with a dark blue blouse with ruffles down the front. I told the girls when I texted them that Simon had paid my bar bill, and they both thought this was amusing. Jessica said, "You go, mum, you walk in there and tell him what's what!" I know she's right: I should be more up front with him; but I'm scared I will push him away. But then he technically is already away from me, so, pulling into the car park and seeing everyone walking in, it becomes more real and I can't bring myself to see him, let alone talk to him. I just need to do my work and concentrate on my own well-being. 'Yeah, right, Ruby,' I scoff to myself. 'You know you want to walk in that room and fuck his beautiful brains out; you know you want him to take you over that big oak desk one more time.' I smile at the thought.

"Good morning," I call through, as I hang my jacket and walk to my desk.

"Good morning, Ruby," says Cecile, as she comes from the kitchen with her coffee. She looks good for her age. "Ruby," she continues, "I must say what you said in that meeting with Runaway Lingerie was fantastic and you really gave them what for." She laughs. "And I've been getting some very good feedback from them. They loved how open you were, and there are even talks of doing a special line just for the, um, larger ladies," she says in a whisper, then smiles. "How exciting!" she adds.

"Cecile," I say with joy in my voice, "this is fantastic news. I'm so chuffed they like my ideas." I really am feeling pleased with myself.

She hugs her mug, smiles, and says, "I know, right?" then walks off like she knows some big secret. She can be so intelligent at times and yet so young at heart.

I sit on my chair and fly off into a daydream of ad campaigns and photoshoots, with me as the top director. Wow, if only, Ruby! My phone rings and it's Simon. Fuck, here goes, let's spoil Ruby's day with some headfuck game. I pick up the handset and speak with a clear voice, "Good morning, Mr Hails," and I know he will be smiling at that.

He replies with, "Hello, Ms Frankton, could you come to my office, please?" and I think, 'Oh, here we go. I love it when I'm right.'

"Yes, sure," I say in a sarcastic manner. "I'll be right in." I replace the handset, take a deep breath, stand and straighten my shirt. It's only 9.45am, and I already have to face the sexy beast. Walking to his office, I pass Mervin, who looks like he's had a haircut, and I can't help but think he looks very handsome in a geeky kind of way. He smiles at me and gives a little wave from his desk.

I knock on Simon's door and enter – no way I'm waiting for a reply. He is already standing by the window, with his arms folded in front of him, wearing some tight-fitting black trousers and a white, long-sleeved shirt with the sleeves rolled up – he looks divine, and I can smell his aftershave. The view out of the window allows you to watch the comings and goings of the people in the petrol station; I have the same view from my window in my part of the building, where I sit feeling lonely most of the day.

I close the door quietly behind me and walk over to one of the red leather chairs and take a seat. He turns to face me and places his hands in his pockets, which makes him look all the more sexy, and I think, 'How can this man make me feel the way he does with just a look?' I'm still angry with him for leaving me alone Friday evening.

"I trust you had a restful weekend?" he asks, and he can't help but smile, the sexy bastard.

"Yes, I did, thank you very much," I reply in a sweet yet pissy voice.

"Good," he says, "because now I need your help.

"Wait, what did you say? You need my help?" I can't help but laugh.

"Yes," he replies, "I need your help getting the Runaway Lingerie's Naughty But Nice line up and running."

"Wait a minute, what do you mean, you need my help? Simon, I don't know how to run a lingerie line, or any line for that matter," I say, standing. "What do you mean, I have to help?"

He holds out his hands and tells me to calm down. "Ruby, we think you have some amazing ideas." He swallows. "We want your input into launching the new line, aimed at getting larger people feeling and looking sexy – and let's face it, you're not afraid to speak out and tell people what you think about this subject. We want real people looking one hundred percent real, wearing our lingerie range," he continues.

"Our range?" I say, all confused.

"Yes," he replies, "we have decided to invest a lot more and we will have a share of all profits, and as we are the main advertiser of the brand, we will get a good deal out of it. After all, that's how it works; and don't panic, because I will be with you every step of the way – you have my word on that. Plus, you have the whole team at your disposal," he says, as he points in the direction of the other office, "and if we can launch this range with the profits we are predicting, we stand to make a lot of money; and, of course" – he smiles – "you will be rewarded financially for your hard work." He finally takes a breath and I can see the passion in his eyes.

I look at him with a straight face and shake my head. "Simon," I finally say in a low voice, "I've never done anything like this in my life; I'm not sure I would even know where to start. Plus, I'm just a receptionist! There must be other people who can do this better than me."

He steps closer and pulls my arms so that they are now around him. His touch drives me crazy, as he leans down and kisses me ever so softly on the lips, and with that oh-so-sexy voice he says, "You've got this. I wouldn't ask if I didn't think you could do it. You are the best person for this job," and with that, he kisses me again long and soft, with all lips and tongues, and I melt into him, like the weekend has faded away and I'm not hurting any more.

We finally pull apart and he asks me to at least think about it, to which I say I will. I step back and want to get away from him, but only because I want more, and it's just not right when we are at work. I tell him I need to get back to work, and he says with his head dipped, "I understand; but please think about coming on board. We could even draw up a contract if that would help," he adds.

"Simon, I need to get back to work. I promise I will spend the rest of the week thinking about it." I'm a little sad to leave his office, as I need to ask him so many questions, but now is not the time. I can see things will only end bad if I stay; plus, I need to collect my thoughts.

"Sorry," he mumbles. "I'll let you get back to work."

I head for the door and stop. I turn back to ask him, "Why did you pay my bar bill, Simon?"

He lifts his head up from the pc where he now sits, and smiles. "Hey, we are friends, aren't we?" He winks at the same time.

Wow, a winking, playful Simon! That's who I'm falling deeply in love with, not this cold-leave-me-in-a-stairwell-alone-after-hot-sex Simon, so I smile back at him and say, "Yes, Simon, but you're also my boss." This makes him smile.

I turn and leave the room, heading back to my desk to do some work. He is impossible to be around. I just need to take every day as it comes. I sigh, sitting back at my desk.

The rest of the day is gone all too quickly. I can't concentrate; I have lots of decisions to make, and I know it's going to be a rollercoaster of emotion – the biggest one being, am I good enough?

So when the girls come over Wednesday evening for pizza and I tell them all about the offer, Belle is practically jumping for joy. "My god, mum," she says, "this is amazing, and you should definitely go for it."

Jessica says the same. "Mum, what have you got to lose?" she cries. "You have gone from pub bouncer to shop supervisor to assistant manager to receptionist – what makes you think you can't do this?" She carries on, "You dress smart and you know what women want." She smiles. "Mum, you've got this!

You're amazing!" This makes me smile, and I know they mean well, but it's that exact word, *lose*, that makes me shudder. What if I fail? What if I say no: will Simon move on to someone else? Will he fire me? So many questions.

Both the girls stay late and we talk about the ifs and buts of my promotion, so to speak, never really coming to a conclusion, and by ten o'clock I'm so tired from it all I tell them I'm going to bed. I see them out of the house and safely in their car, with a wave and an 'I love you'. I watch them drive away, shut the door and turn the key – I am once again alone. I climb the stairs, turning off lights as I go, I clean my teeth and crawl into bed. I grab my air pods and search up a good song on my phone: Cyndi Lauper's 'Time After Time' seems like a good choice. I soon fall into a peaceful sleep, while congratulating myself on not having a drink. I actually can't remember the last time I didn't have a drink.

Thursday rolls into Friday and Friday rolls into Saturday. I hate the weekends, because I'm alone. The girls announce they are off to Greece in a few weeks for a last-minute bargain holiday; I'm so envious of them, but I would never let them know that. I'm super-proud of them both. If I could fit in their suitcase, I would.

CHAPTER ELEVEN

I've had a lazy day doing sod all, thinking of Simon and wishing he would text me, and before I know it seven thirty has crept around. I've been shopping today and stocked up on the essentials such as vodka. I even managed to buy some fresh fruit, so that after my dinner I can have some strawberries and squirty cream. Oh how exciting my life is!

Later, I watch a movie on Netflix about a woman who is blind: she falls in love with her neighbor, who turns out to be a serial killer, and she has to fight to survive when he takes her out in a wood for a camping trip. I can't help but think, good luck with that one; no way would I go camping, let alone camping when I was blind. In the end, I'm not really paying much attention. I've had quite a lot of vodka at this point, because drowning my sorrows is all I seem to do lately.

Suddenly, there is a loud knock at the door, which makes me bloody jump. I put down my drink, get up and go the window – in the darkness of the street I can see a figure and I can instantly tell it's Simon, looking all hot and sexy. "What the fucking hell is he doing here?" I say through gritted teeth, while in my head

I'm screaming, 'Holy fuck, he's here, again, another headfuck game to be played.' I walk to the door and open it in an aggressive manner and he jumps back as if I scared him. He smiles, but I'm not having any of it, so with my arms folded and an angry look on my face, I yell, "What on earth are you doing here?"

He steps forward. He's calm and smiling, and tries to put a hand on my face, but I instantly step back. He stops and looks puzzled, like someone has taken his favourite toy away. "Ruby, have I done something wrong?"

I look at him in utter disbelief. "Have you done something wrong, Simon?" I say all bitchy like.

He pushes forward and closes the door behind him. "Ruby, I don't understand," he says. "If this is about what happened in the hotel…"

"Well, if you don't know now, you never will," I snap. "You can't keep coming in and out of my life like this. You can't play with me like I'm a toy you just think you can toss away when you get your fill!" I shout, the alcohol making me brave.

He tries to come closer and I step back again. He smiles. "See, this is what I love about you, Ruby — your passion," he teases, with eyes wide.

"Look, you need to leave. I'm not in the mood for all your bullshit tonight," I say in a very harsh, maybe too harsh voice, and with that I start climbing the stairs. I need some distance, but I'm instantly aware he's following me. "I'm serious, Simon; you need to go."

He starts climbing the stairs after me and I know I need to get away from him. I sprint the rest of the way up the stairs and into the bathroom, closing the door behind me. I lock it and step back against the sink. He tries to come in, begging me to open the door. "This is crazy," he shouts, but I scream at him to please leave. "Ruby Frankton, open this door!" he yells, and he sounds mad.

"No, Simon, I won't. You will have to fucking break it down," I cry. "Please, just leave, Simon." I'm so angry: how dare he come here so late and just expect a warm welcome?

"Ruby," he shouts, "so help me god, if I break down this fucking door I'm going to fuck you into the middle of next week, and I promise you won't walk for a month!" Oh, shouty Simon, how dominant; and with that, my heart does a flip – but I'm not giving in.

"Well then, I'm guessing you should fucking break it down," I goad.

"Ruby Frankton, just remember, you asked for it," he says in a threatening but playful way; and with that, I hear his foot hit the door and it springs open, banging against the wall, making me jump and leaving a dent. I don't have time to react before he lunges at me, grabbing me around my waist.

I scream, "Simon, don't you dare!" I cry out for him to get off, but he's not listening. He picks me up and throws me over his shoulder, and my god is he strong? I pound on his back like a gorilla beating its chest, screaming to be put down, but he doesn't care. He walks to my room and throws me on the bed. I instantly try to make a run for it, but he pushes me back down and in one swift move my sweatpants are off. "Simon, please," I beg him, "this isn't fair." But he's ignoring me.

He undoes his own trousers and again I make a run for it, until we end up fighting on the bedroom floor, and he rips at my thong, biting my arse cheek. I crawl away, getting as far as the bedroom door; then I feel him grab me from behind, making me cry out in anger. "Simon, no!" I scream, but he picks me up again and throws me back on the bed, pulling my thong off and throwing it across the room. I am naked from the waist down, and as I roll over to face him, he's got his own trousers off and his huge hard cock is swinging free. I try to push past him, but he's just too strong, and he pounces on top of me, pulling both my arms above my head and spreading my legs apart using his knee. I'm struggling and calling his name, but he's not listening or talking – he's not said one word to me, and he's on a mission, and it's so sexy.

"Please," I beg him, but he's there at my entrance, and before I can finish saying his name, he has filled me deep and hard. I cry out in pleasure and frustration, trying to move, but my arms are pinned. How can I keep letting him do this to me? But I already know the answer: because I want him to. I want him so badly, I can't stand it.

All the while he is pounding me, harder and harder, he's making the most sexiest noises. He releases my arms and pulls my top up tugging it over my head, and he grabs my left breast with his right hand. He bites my nipple hard and I cry out again. This is too much! My head is going to explode!

His left hand is gripping my hair and I hit him with closed fists on his back and say his name with a deep sigh. Fuck me, he feels good – but he just keeps going. After a few more thrusts, he releases his load deep inside me, groaning wildly and through gritted teeth, saying, "You will be the death of me, Ruby Frankton."

He feels so good when he comes, like really good, and I try to catch my breath as we lay there for a while. I can't believe that just happened. He is a hot mess breathing hard on my chest, and I tug his hair, trying to get a reaction, and I finally say, "Simon, this isn't fair how you keep blowing hot and cold with me. You can't just pick me up and put me down whenever you feel like it." I try to push him off me, and he moves on to his hands, hovering above my face. His eyes look sad, like he's hiding a deep dark secret and it's drowning him from the inside.

"I'm sorry," he finally says. "I'm not good with this sort of thing," and with that, he pulls out of me, making me gasp, and sits on the edge of the bed, putting on his trousers. I get up, grab my t-shirt and move past him. I need to go to the bathroom, and as I sit and pee, I can see the lock on my bathroom door is completely hanging off, which makes me smile. I flush the toilet and wash my hands.

He appears at the bathroom door fully dressed, and I turn to face him, leaning on the sink with my hands holding the basin behind me. I say in a calm voice, "So you're leaving again."

He steps into the bathroom and leans against the wall. "Ruby, I can't stay. I wish I could," he continues, "but I can't. I'm sorry."

I stand up from the sink and I pull my t-shirt down to cover my modesty. Speaking clearly and in a controlled voice, I say, "Then I guess you'd better leave." My face is completely straight, and he drops his head and gives a muffled grumble through gritted teeth, which sounded like good one Simon, and he runs his hand through his hair. "Simon," I repeat, "I need you to leave." My eyes are full of tears, but I won't let them flow – I can't let them flow. He cannot see me cry, he cannot know this is killing me.

"Ruby, I'm sorry." He then nods as if accepting his fate and turns to walk out of the door, heading for the stairs; then he turns back to look at me, and I'm screaming in my head for him to leave, but at the same time I want him to stay and hold me and tell me he loves me and that he wants to be with me. He gives me a half-cocked smile, shakes his head and walks the rest of the way down the stairs and out of the front door, and only when I hear it shut do I collapse on the floor and sob.

I haven't cried like this for years, but I cry with heavy tears and the feeling of not being good enough. I have never felt so lonely and used and unwanted in my life – even my ex-husband wanted me more than Simon, and that's saying something. My thoughts are racing. I need a drink, I need to sink into oblivion and whatever this is, what we have, has to stop.

I scramble back to my feet and blow my nose and I go find my thong and sweatpants. My bed now is a mess of where we just were, but I head downstairs to find my vodka – this is what I need, this is my friend. I drink the rest of the bottle, then stumble back up to bed.

Sunday morning comes and goes and I'm feeling pretty damn hungover. I don't get up. It's now just before mid-day, but I can't face the world. I hear the front door open and a big "Hey, mum" from the living room. It's Belle. I don't get up or shout back, because my head hurts when I move. "Mum?" I hear again, as she gets closer to my room. "Mum?" she shouts as she crashes into my room.

I look up at her from my bed and just pull the covers back over my head. I just want to die. "Mum," she says, sitting on the bed, "what the hell is going on? I have been calling you all morning, and Jessica is worried sick."

Shit, I totally forgot to charge my phone last

night; in actual fact, I don't even know where my phone is. "I'm so sorry," I tell her in a low, apologetic tone. "I had a bit too much to drink last night." I look at her full of guilt.

"I'm guessing, by the look of you," she giggles, "you had a lot to drink last night." Why do I feel like I'm being told off? "Mum," she sighs, "talk to me, tell me what's going on. I want to help."

I feel my eyes well up, but I can't tell her about Simon; I don't want anyone to know how I've let yet another man make me feel this way.

"Is it money?" she adds.

I shake my head slowly. "No," I say. I'm financially sound, and it's true I've never been so well off; with the divorce settlement due in the bank and my new wage packet coming in, I'm actually well off – well, I feel well off compared to most.

"Is it a man?" she says in a more serious voice and with a concerned look on her face. "Is it your boss?"

Yes, I scream in my head, yes, it is a fucking man, and yes, it's my fucking boss; but I don't say it out loud. I just shake my head slowly and attempt to sit up.

She stands up and says, "Well, I'm going to make you a super-strong coffee and when you're ready you can come down and tell me all about it, yeah?" – as if to say, 'I'm not leaving until you tell me why you're in bed with a massive hangover, and in a real bad state.'

Okay, I nod, fair play: she wants to know her mum is okay, and I need to tell her something so she won't worry.

"Oh, and I'll tell Jessica that Sunday roast is off, shall I?" she says with a screwed-up face. "And I'll tell her you're feeling unwell, yeah?" She smiles and leaves the room.

I drag myself to the bathroom and look in the mirror. 'My god,' says my inner disappointment, 'I told you so; like, yeah, I really told you!' I wash my face and clean my teeth because my mouth feels wretched. I slowly walk downstairs as if I was broken and head for the kitchen, where Belle places a coffee mug full of dark hot coffee on the kitchen table and tells me to sit. "I would rather have a cup of tea," I tell her.

She gives me a look of 'well, it's coffee, so drink it', so I do as I'm told, because I need to sit before I fall. She sits opposite me and hugs her mug in both hands with her elbows resting on the table. I pick up my mug and take a tiny sip; it tastes strong, but I know I need it. I look at her like, 'okay, okay, I'll tell you, just give me a minute.' She just sits silently, waiting for me to speak. I sit back in my chair and with both hands tightly around my mug, I proceed to tell her that I was feeling lonely and not having a friend to talk to any more, which just, well, made me angry and sad and thankful all at the same time, and before I knew it I had drunk a whole bottle of vodka. I smile – well, a half-smile.

She looks at me through squinted eyes. "Why do I feel you're not telling the whole truth?" she says. "Is that why the bathroom door lock is hanging off?"

"Belle, I've just got a lot going on with work at the minute, and I just let it get on top of me, that's all; and yes, I kicked the bathroom door in anger," and as I say that, I think of Simon between my legs, lying on top of me, and I smile.

She looks at me and smiles back. "Okay," she says, "but you would tell me if you needed my help, yeah?"

I sigh and say, "Yes, sweetheart, you and Jessica are my world."

"Good," she giggles, "now get yourself off up to bed and recover, you raging alcoholic."

I laugh hard, but it hurts my head so I stop. I stand slowly and walk through the lounge and up the stairs to bed, and once in bed, it's where I stay till Monday morning.

CHAPTER TWELVE

The next three weeks go by in a blur. I've made it clear to Simon I want to get this launch party out of the way before we decide what's going on with whatever this is between us, as much as I want him to do dirty things to me over and over again.

He nods when I tell him, with his hands in his pockets and a big 'I wanna fuck you so bad' smile on his face; but he says he understands, which, to my surprise, is a breath of fresh air.

We have meeting upon meeting with Runaway Lingerie, and I hate meetings, because everyone keeps asking me to stand up and speak, and I really feel I've said all I need to say; but no, they want more, like blood-sucking vampires needing a fix.

We design websites and come up with slogans for the new advert; we advertise for women to interview for the cover of our lingerie magazine – now this is an area I'm most interested in, because I want it to be right: we want real people, and real people is what we will get; we predict profits and negotiate prices; and when the final line is ready, I can't contain my excitement. I'm so proud of myself for my achievements. Larger models from across Norfolk applied to be in our show: they all want to wear our new line.

My girls are super-excited for me – well, for everyone really – but they can't stop telling me how proud they are of me. The collection is fantastic and I can't wait for the launch party next week. We have some lovely models wanting to show off the line, which is super-cool.

When Saturday comes, I call the girls and we head out to celebrate. They arrive at mine all dressed up, and they always look super-pretty. Jessica is like me, with blonde hair, and Belle is like her dad, with dark hair; but you can see they are sisters, and that makes me smile. We head for the local Rose & Thorn pub – it's local and less rough – and we grab some drinks from the bar and head out in the afternoon sun without a care in the world.

Simon has not tried to touch me or message me for weeks, and it's been kind of lovely, but also very difficult. A few times we were alone and the sexual tension between us is there, and is hard to deny, but I've stood my ground and made it clear that he needed to back off and leave me alone. As much as it saddened me, I know it is for the best – at least while we are at work.

"Guys," I say, "I can't believe I'm not going to see you for a whole two weeks," I tell them, leaning against the sticky bar after way too many drinks, waiting for another round.

"It's Greece, mum, not New Zealand," laughs Belle. "We will be back before you know it."

I sigh hard and say, "I know, but dropping you off at the airport tomorrow is going to be super-hard for me."

They both hug me and we dance the night away to the local band that's playing cheesy eighties songs. It's gone midnight when the taxi drops me off first and I tell them I will pick them up at three o'clock sharp tomorrow. "Okay, mum," they shout. "Love you!" they scream as the taxi drives away.

I walk inside, shut the door and collapse on the sofa. In my drunken state, I feel like sending Simon a text, but when I come to sending it, I just roll over and fall asleep.

Sunday morning, I wake with a sore head, but soon freshen up with a shower and a tea. Grabbing my phone, I'm in shock when I see a message from Simon. He says that, guessing from the message I sent, I was drunk and we can discuss it on Monday. Oh shit! What did I send? I scroll up and read it back: 'Simoom where's area Youku I neeEd u.' Oh, fuck! What the hell, Ruby, how fucking drunk was I? I didn't think I sent it. What a dick – and wow, we will discuss it Monday!

I can't worry about it now, as I have to take the girls to the airport. Three o'clock comes and I'm outside the girls' house. honking my horn. "Come on, girls!" I shout. "We will be late." I don't like taking my car on long journeys as she is old, let alone leave her running unnecessarily. They pack the boot and we head off in the direction of the airport, the three hour journey filled with laughter and singing. My girls are the funniest people I've ever met – they must take after me.

The roads are clear and we get there nice and early, despite all the worry. I drop them off outside terminal four, as the parking is way too overpriced; they grab their bags and I hug them both and tell them to have an amazing time. Jessica's best friend is waving desperately in the departures entrance.

"We will, mum," says Belle.

"Yeah, mum, we will," says Jessica. "Just try not to worry," she adds, and as they walk away I can't help but worry and I can't help but feel alone again. It's a feeling I've become accustomed to.

They both turn and wave as they disappear through the sliding doors, and I climb back into my car and head home, listening to Chaka Khan's 'Ain't Nobody', and singing with all my might. I need to get home and just chill and not worry all night; like I know I'm going to, but then again they are big girls now, and I know they will have each other.

Forty minutes from home and I notice the temperature on my car has hit an all-time high and a red warning light comes on. "Oh, no, please just get me home!" I shout. I can't break down now. But one more mile and she's done: she just splutters and stops.

I manage to pull over into a layby and I put my head on the steering wheel. 'Now what, Ruby?' I say to myself, as I look in the rear-view mirror. I pull out my phone and think about who I can call. It's Sunday evening, and I don't think a recovery truck will come out, and I don't have roadside assistance. Great, Ruby, well done! I close my eyes and the only name that pops into my head is Simon's – and I'm shaking my head in utter dismay. How convenient, Ruby! I find his name on my phone under 'Can't commit', and press the call button. He answers straight away.

"Ruby, hi," he says all sexy. "What's wrong?" he adds.

"Simon, I'm sorry to bother you, but my car has broken down and I don't know who else to call."

"Hey," he says, "it's fine. Tell me where you are and I'll come collect you."

Wow, I wasn't expecting that! I explain I'm in a layby about thirty-five miles from work on the A11 just past Attleborough, coming back from the airport. He gives me a brief description of where he thinks I am and I'm amazed he knows what direction to head in.

"I'll be twenty-five minutes," he says. "Just stay in your car and wait for me."

"Well, yeah," I say, "where else am I meant to go?" I laugh, and he says 'bye' and hangs up. I have a feeling this is a bad idea, but what other choice do I have? 'Who else could I have called?' I think. 'My ex-husband,' laughs my inner cow. Yeah, I can imagine the look on my ex-best friend's face as he says, 'I'm off to rescue my ex-wife.'

I wait for just over thirty minutes and it's very dark outside. The roads are empty and this creeps me out a little, but all of a sudden I see lights pull up behind me and I can see it's a black Range Rover Sport. 'Wow, nice car!' I say to myself, looking in the mirror, and I know it's him. He steps out all sexy and hot looking in his navy blue jeans and a casual white t-shirt. Wow, he looks like fucking sex on legs! He walks over and I climb out of my car to meet him. He asks me if I'm okay and I say 'yes'. He tells me he's called the tow company and they will collect my car in the morning and take it to the garage across the road from work.

"Wow," I say, "that was nice of you."

He tilts his head and says, "I have my uses."

I smile back and say, "Well, thank you, but I just need to get home." It's a lie: I have nothing to get home for.

He smiles back and says, "I understand."

I gather my things and lock my car, and he walks me to my side of his car and opens the door for me. What a gentleman, I think, as I take in his delicious smell. He shuts my door and walks back to his side of the car while I take a quick glance in the back to see if there is any evidence of a child or something that would suggest a woman has been in here – but there is nothing.

He climbs in and starts the car, turning down the stereo, which is playing Paloma Faith's 'Only Love Can Hurt Like This', and I think, 'Oh, how appropriate.' It really is a nice car, all black leather seats and cream trimmings, and as we start to drive, neither one of us speaks. He glances at me briefly, and I glance back; the electricity between us is unbearable, and the heat in the car is fucking hot.

We turn onto the A47 towards the back of Taverham to my house; there are fields on either side of us and the roads are dead. Eventually, he says, "What was that message all about last night?"

I sigh a long sigh and say, "Sorry, I was drunk. I wasn't going to send it, but I must have pressed 'send' as I was falling asleep," I add. "Just pretend I didn't send it. It's not like you care anyway."

Suddenly, he shouts, "For fuck's sake, Ruby! Fuck this," and he swings off the road onto a track that leads to the back of some farm buildings.

He comes to a halt and I yell, "What the hell are you doing, Simon?"

He just grabs the wheel and says, "I can't stand this between us, Ruby. You won't come near me, and it's doing my head in. Then you send me drunk messages and then you tell me to pretend it doesn't matter."

"Well I'm sorry, Simon," I shout, "but I don't care any more" – and I know that's a lie, because I care a lot; I fucking care so much it hurts. "You're hot and cold with me, and now it's my turn to be cold with you; so please take me home." He doesn't move. "Please take me home." I stare at him.

He shakes his head and says, "Not until we sort this."

"For fuck's sake, Simon," I say, "there is nothing to sort. You won't open up to me, you won't tell me anything about you, and you fucking ignore me – yet you want to still fuck me and then walk away," and as I finish what I'm saying I grab the door handle, adding, "Fine, I will walk home," and with that I exit the car, slamming the door shut behind me, and I start to walk around to the boot. The evening air is warm, and there is nobody in sight, just lights in the distance. Determined to leave, I head for the main road; then I hear him slam his door and before I can do anything he's in front of me.

"Ruby, stop," he snaps, trying to grab me, and I slap his face with my left hand. This shocks him, and I raise my right hand, ready to strike again. He grabs it, swinging me around to the side of the car. I hit out at him and tell him this is not happening again, to which he replies, "Oh yes it fucking is!"

He holds both of my wrists tightly above my head with his left hand so they are flat against the car, and I cry out in pain, trying to push him away with my body. He uses his free hand to undo my jeans and yank them down enough for his hand to fit down the front towards my now throbbing vagina. I yell out, as if this will make him stop, and I try to shout for help, although I don't mean it. He kisses me hard and I bite his lip; he smiles, but carries on. His hand has found my sweet spot and I can't help but give in a little and I stop my struggling, as I feel his fingers touch my clit. He releases my hands and he grabs my arse hard. I finger his hair and we kiss with a new desperate need. He slips his fingers inside, and I moan into his mouth. He removes his hand and with both hands free, he pulls down my jeans and thong, while my shoes go flying, and with his hair brushing past my delicate area, I feel so horny. I pull one leg out of my jeans and his face goes for the soft warm spot between my legs, his tongue exploring my wet folds. I am lost in the moment: I am in heaven. He is licking me over and over, again and again, outside in the open where anyone could see. I pull his hair and he moans loudly – this alone sends me over the edge and I'm coming hard. I cry out into the evening sky, saying 'fuck' over and over again.

He stands and opens the back door of the car and in one swift move he pushes me down on my front, kicking my legs apart, and I can hear him yank his jeans undone. I can't stand the wait; I'm practically begging for him to fuck me – and in less than a second he's inside me. He pulls my hair and I arch my back and call out in surprise. He's rough, but not too rough; I love it, I need it, I want him, I need him. He makes a low moaning sound between gritted teeth and fucks me harder than before, my hips forced into the black leather seats, and I cry out again and again. I feel him getting rock hard and he's moving faster and I know he's close. I feel the soft leather under my palms as I grab at the seat, and I call out with heated breath, "Simon, please," and this undoes him: he fills me with his sticky salty liquid, his movements eventually slowing, and finally he collapses on my back. We are both breathing hard, him from his orgasm, and me from his weight.

He finally stands, and I slowly lift myself up, my body stiff. I feel numb and I can't face him; I can't let him see my flushed face. I'm angry at myself because I let him do this to me again, and I shake my head. I need to walk away. He's flushed and catching his breath while doing his jeans back up and running his hand through his hair, so I pull up my thong and jeans. "Simon, I can't do this again," I say in a delicate voice. He stares at me in shock, like he can't believe what he just did. "I can't be here," I add, and I start walking – I walk away from him, and I don't even bother to grab my shoes. I feel drunk, I feel despair.

He calls out after me, but I don't listen; he calls and calls, but I keep walking, stumbling along the dirt track in the dark. I hear him shut his car door and start his engine, spinning his car around so he is now alongside me. He rolls down the passenger window and says, "Ruby, please get in." I ignore him. "Please,

Ruby, please," he is begging.

I stop and look at him – well, I look past him. "Take me home, Simon," I say with tears in my eyes.

"Please get in, Ruby," he says once more. "I'm sorry. I will take you home," he adds, so I grab the handle, open the door and climb in. He doesn't move for a few seconds, as if trying to figure out what to do. "Please speak, Ruby," he pleads; but I do not speak. I am silent and emotional, so he starts to drive slowly down the track towards the main road "Ruby, please, please talk to me; you're scaring me," he adds.

The tears fall from my eyes and all I can do is quietly sob. He drives me the rest of the ten minutes to my home and parks right outside my door, then comes round to my side of the car and helps me out. My body aches. He finds my keys from my bag and we walk silently across the pavement. He unlocks the door and he walks me in, shutting the door behind us, then takes me straight upstairs. We walk into the bathroom and he sits me on the toilet seat, opens the shower curtain and turns on the shower, kneeling in front of me. I can see the look of pain on his face is sincere, as he wipes the tears from my face. I lean my head into his hand. How can this beautiful man make me feel so helpless?

I can't stop sobbing and I know I must look a mess and a little bit crazy, as he pulls my top up over my head and I lift my arms to help him, and with one hand he unhooks my bra, sliding it down my arms to reveal my soft breasts. He gets me to stand and undoes my jeans, all the while looking deep inside me. I don't say a word as he pulls down my jeans and my now wet thong and helps me to step out of them. He removes his own t-shirt and kicks off his shoes – he has the most beautiful body. He helps me step into the shower and without removing his own jeans, he comes in behind me and lowers me down so I'm sitting with my back against his chest, my head resting on his collar bone. The water is warm on my skin, and he wraps his arms around me and squeezes me tight. I let the sobs come in loud, sharp bursts, my body convulsing, but he never lets me go, not even a little bit. We just stay there in my shower for what seems forever.

Simon gently whispers, "I'm so, so sorry, Ruby," over and over again, until the shower has gone cold and I'm starting to shiver, so he reaches up, moving me forward, and turns off the water. He grabs a towel from the rail on the wall beside us, stands up and gets out of the shower. I lean back against the now cold bath as he strips out of his soaking wet jeans and tosses them on the floor in the corner; then, helping me to stand, he wraps the towel around my shoulders, gently rubbing me dry. He is so gentle and kind, and he just keeps saying sorry.

He then guides me into my bedroom and dries the rest of me. I feel like a child, but I have just detached myself from the situation; plus, deep down somewhere, I'm loving all the attention. He gently dries my hair and wraps the towel back around me to cover me up, like he knows that's what I would want. My eyes never leave his, as he places his hand on either side of my face and he kisses me. I kiss him back because, for some reason, I still fucking want him – after everything, I still want him.

We share a slow and sensual kiss. I know he's trying hard to make things right, and this makes my heart swell. Removing my towel, happy that I'm dry, he bends down and opens the covers to my bed and he helps me slide in. It's warm and cosy, and it's where I want to be. I look up at him in desperation, but he smiles and whispers close to my ear, "I'm not going anywhere tonight, Ruby."

I lay down with my head on my soft pillow and he dries himself with the same towel and then climbs in behind me and wraps his arms around me once more, my head now resting on his arm. I can feel his chest on my back and his gentle breathing, his warm skin on mine: this feels like heaven. We are totally naked and free, and this feels like love, this feels like it could be a strong love. I feel myself drift off into a peaceful sleep, not caring for the rest of this night.

CHAPTER THIRTEEN

I wake with a start, almost falling out of the bed, but then I realise he is still here, because I can feel his heat and hear him breathing; so I turn carefully to face him. I'm in utter shock that this beautiful man is still lying next to me. He is fast asleep on his back, and I rest my head on my elbow so his outstretched arm is under my body, and I stare at his beautiful face, his nose, his eyes, his lips, memorising every detail. My eyes wander down his now-exposed chest: his tattoo is very big and full of black ink swirls, and there is not a single hair to be seen, no scars, no evidence he's ever been hurt. I run my finger down his tight stomach towards his groin and he stirs. This makes me giggle and I have to put my hand to my mouth to stop it being loud; but this makes him stir even more. He slowly rolls over to face me and, not opening his eyes, says, "Good morning, Ruby."

I inhale deeply and lay my head down on his arm next to his head and say in a cheeky voice, "Good morning, Mr Hails," and with that, he opens his eyes and mouth wide as if in shock.

He grabs me, pulling me on top of him, yelling, "Come here, you cheeky little shit!"

I laugh hard as we roll over. He tickles me, not letting up, turning me over on to my back so he is now positioned between my legs, resting on his elbow. I look into his eyes and say, "Sorry for last night. I don't know what happened."

He kisses me hard, he kisses me for a long time; we are tangled together, with my legs around his waist, and he finally stops and looks at me and says, "No, Ruby, it is I who is sorry. I have treated you unfairly and what I did last night was cruel and barbaric. Please forgive me, I beg you."

Wow, this is unexpected! My mind is racing, Simon saying he was genuinely sorry. I can definitely use this against him at some point. He kisses me again, but this feels different, like he wants to be here, he needs to be here, and he is starting to feel something. Maybe I'm reading too much into it, maybe he was just on auto-pilot and it's what he does to all his women.

I feel him slide his hard cock inside me and we make love – I mean actual love: he is so tender and gentle with me; we are naked and free, and all arms and legs and open to possibilities, rotating his hips so he can feel every inch of me. I run my hands down his spine and feel his smooth buttocks, as he moans with pleasure, and I am happy for the first time in months – mind-blowingly happy. All the memories from last night fade away.

When he finally lets go, it's with a calm low

growl and I love it: this is the Simon I want and need. We lay in each other's arms, not wanting to move, with me stroking his back and fingering his hair, and after a few short minutes he eventually looks up at me and gives me a cheesy grin and slides out of me and I wince. He looks shocked and asks in a concerned voice, "Oh my god, did I hurt you?"

"No," I reply, shaking my head. "I'm just a bit sore, and my body aches from the position you had me in." I smile. "It's a pleasurable pain, I promise." He still looks concerned. "I promise I'm fine," I say.

He kisses me and grins, saying, "Okay."

"Simon?" I say in a quizzical manner.

"Yes, Ruby?" he says as he's kissing my neck. I go silent and he looks up at me. "What is it?" he says.

I give him a big smile and say, "I need to pee, and we need to get ready for work."

He lets out a big sigh and says, "Fuck work, we are having the day off!" He puts his head on my chest and says, "I just want to be here with you," and I can't help but giggle. He moves off me, trying to be gentle, and rolls over on his back, and I slide out of the bed and out of the room to use the loo. I see my clothes on the floor and shake my head, and then his jeans in the corner in a crumpled mess, and I smile.

I wipe myself – yes, I'm definitely sore – then I flush the toilet and wash my hands. I decide to hang his jeans on the heated rail to dry, and return to him in the bedroom. He's still lying there, all sexy and beautiful, and I jump inside with delight. Leaning on the doorframe, I give the biggest smile.

He sees me smile and asks, "What's so funny, Ms Frankton?"

I say, "Oh, nothing," while leaping in the air and throwing myself on top of him. He grabs my sides and we roll around the bed, trying to pin each other down. It truly is a teenager-type moment.

We stay in bed for most of the day and we talk about last night and how it made me feel. I tell him, "I love the chase, don't get me wrong; I love the thrill of the chase. We are having fucking fantastic sex, and never in my wildest dreams did I ever think I would meet someone and fall in love again," and as I say it, I look straight at him. Shit, I think, I said it out loud.

He smiles and kisses my forehead, as if trying to soften the blow of him not saying it back; then he tells me in a soft voice, "Love is a complicated feeling, and I've tried to stay away from it my whole life." He gives a deep sigh, and I truly understand why he would. I mean, look at him and look at what he's had to deal with in the last twenty-four hours: for one, he had to deal with all my emotions and shit. I wouldn't want to entertain it if I was a sex god like him; I would want to be free and do as I please and not have commitments. He squeezes me tight and says, "I'm happy the way things are," and I think to myself, 'But what does that mean? Happy to just fuck me when he feels likes it and then leave me happy, or happy he's in my bed right now happy?' He is so confusing, but I'm not going to probe deeper now because I don't want to spoil this moment. For now I'm happy, and that will do.

We both decide we need to eat and so he gets up and walks out of the room stark bollock naked. I call after him and ask him what he's doing, but I don't hear him answer. Oh, shit, I instantly think to myself, he's done it again – he's fucking left me. So I decide to get up and go see where he is. As I peek into the bathroom, I can still see his jeans hanging on the rail and instantly feel relief. I can hear a lot of banging going on from the kitchen, so I walk back to my room, open my closet and put on a long white off-the-shoulder t-shirt. I contemplate putting a thong on, but decide against it; so, feeling sexy and brave, I head downstairs to where he is, and as I stand in the doorway to my kitchen, I get a beautiful image of Simon looking in my cupboards for something, and oh my god, does he look fuckable!

He spins around when he hears my feet shuffle, and flashes me the biggest smile. He puts down on the counter what I see is flour and walks over to me in the doorway, wrapping his arms around my waist and slowly moving them down to my behind, and he smiles when he reaches my plump bottom, realising I'm not wearing any underwear. "Well now, then, Ms Frankton, what do we have here?" he teases, slowly lifting my shirt so he can place his palms on my bare bum. He kisses me hard, pushing my back against the doorframe, bringing his hands up and around to my front, and sliding them up the inside of my t-shirt until he reaches my breasts. I can feel his hard cock pressed against my groin, and I reach my own hands around to his perfect arse and squeeze, pulling him closer into me. He gently squeezes both my breasts, tugging on my nipples, and I moan with delight. He tastes so good, his tongue doing its magic thing, and we are lost in each other. He removes his hands from my shirt and smacks my butt with his right hand, pulling away from me at the same time.

"Hey," I say, "I was enjoying that," while making a sad face.

He smiles and says, "Well I, my dear, am hungry, and if I'm going to fuck you again before I leave, which you know I will, I need some food in my belly," and with that he slaps his own stomach, turns and walks back to the flour and finds a bowl.

I giggle and take a seat at the kitchen table. "So what's on the menu today?" I ask, resting my chin on my fist. He really is a delight to watch.

"Well," he replies, turning around, and I can't help but look at his cock and smile. "This," he says, pointing to his dick, "this is for dessert." He smiles,

"Oh, yummy!" I say all playful. "My god, why does it have to be for dessert?"

"Because I am making you pancakes, and eggs on French toast, with streaky bacon and maple syrup," he tells me all professional like.

Wow, I think, you go, Jamie Oliver. I watch his every move: he looks like he enjoys being in the kitchen. "Do you cook often?" I ask – maybe he will give me an insight to his life. I'm also thinking, 'I could get used to this.'

"Well, yes," he says, "but I work such long hours, as you're fully aware. I'm hardly ever at home."

Well that wasn't the answer I was hoping for. "So, do you live alone then?" I say cautiously.

He turns again from the stove, smiling, and says, "Yes, Ruby, I live alone," as if trying to ease my mind.

"Oh," I say, looking at the floor. "Yes, of course you do." Now I feel silly for asking.

He plates up my food, which smells amazing, and puts it down in front of me with a knife and fork. He then squats down in front of me, placing his hands on my knees. "Ruby, I'm very much single. I live alone and have done for over eight years, and I don't have children, and I don't think I ever want any, okay?" He reaches up and kisses me quickly, then stands and walks to the other side of the table and sits down to eat the meal he's lovingly prepared. He looks up at me before tucking in and says, "Ruby eat your food,"

I can't help but smile, and say, "Yes, boss."

He smiles back just before popping some food in his mouth: even the way he eats is beautiful. I pick up my fork and eat some pancake – it's super-yummy.

We spend the next ten minutes in silence, each of us watching the other eat. Once we finish, we put our plates in the sink and he takes my hand, leading me through the living room and up the stairs to my bathroom. He turns on the water for the shower and pulls my top over my head, then kisses me, and continues to run kisses down my neck onto my breasts. I grab his hair and give a playful tug, and with a mouthful of breast, he tells me to get in the shower because he's going to fuck me now – and when he says that, I can't contain my excitement.

We enter the shower and it's hot on my skin. He pushes me so my back is against the wall, kissing me with a new need, his hands on my breasts, squeezing gently. I reach my arms around him and run my nails down his back, as he moves his left hand between my legs and finds my clit already pulsating. I cry out as he strokes me with a relentless rhythm, then slips a finger inside me, then out and back on my clit, over and over again, his kisses soft on my lips. The pleasure is too much and I come hard, while pulling his hair and moaning into his kiss. Holding me around my waist with one hand, he uses the other to lift one leg up so it rests on the side of the bath, and with one swift move he is inside me. I cry out in shock and pleasure; he feels so good. He moves in a gentle rhythm, his hips swaying around and around, all the time holding me steady; he is so strong, he has no problem holding us both up, as he takes my breasts in turn and places them in his mouth, flicking my nipples with his tongue. I grab his hair and yank hard, making him moan. He kisses me again: he tastes so sweet, his lips are soft and warm. I cry out loudly; he feels so good, and his moans are getting more aggressive. I feel him get harder as I hold on to his strong shoulders for support and he lets go, moving slowly in and out until his shaking stops. I feel absolutely done; I feel my body is going to collapse. I pull him to me and hold him tight, the water running over us like a soft blanket.

He gently pulls out and looks me in the eye. "Ruby, you are phenomenal, you know that, right?" he breathes.

I just hug him again and pull him close to kiss him, until we release each other and he climbs out of the shower, grabbing a towel. He dries himself, his hard cock poking through the towel, and while I clean between my legs and wash my hair, he just stands patiently waiting. He looks good wrapped in my towel, and he holds out another towel for me to step into; he helps dry my back and my hair, kissing me softly on my shoulder.

As we leave the bathroom, he grabs his jeans from the rail, but they still look wet to me. Back in my room, I look at my messy bed and the evidence that he stayed with me. He pulls on his jeans, tugging at the legs, and I stand there, rooted to the spot, just watching him. I can't help but feel sad he is going to leave. I pull a thong from my drawer and slip it on, grabbing another clean t-shirt from the closet.

Once dressed, he comes over to me and announces that he must leave, and I instantly want to cry. He strokes my cheek and says, "Hey, please don't be sad. This has been a very interesting twenty-four hours, and one I won't forget in a while. Tomorrow is Tuesday," he adds, "and I want you to know you are welcome in my office at any time, especially in that little black skirt." I smile and sigh. "What is it?" he asks.

"Well, if I just come into your office at any time, surely the others will think something is going on?"

He chuckles and kisses me. "What on earth makes you think they don't already know?" he says.

Oh, crap! That was not what I was wanting. Great, now they all think I'm in with the boss. I sigh.

"Look, Ruby," he says with conviction, "who gives a damn what anyone thinks? Let them think whatever," he adds, and I know he's right. "I'm sorry, but I have to go. I've had a really lovely day and I'm sorry for last night." He kisses me with his soft lips, and I smile a half-cocked smile.

"So I'll see you tomorrow, then," I say.

As he heads for the door, he turns and says, "Hey, we are friends, aren't we?"

I nod my head and reply, "Yeah, but you're also my hot boss."

He winks at me and turns, heading out of the

door. He grabs his shoes and t-shirt from the bathroom and heads down the stairs and out the front door. I hear his car door shut and his powerful engine roar into life, and as I look out of my bedroom window, I see him pull away and I watch him till the end of the street like some stalker. "Well, Ruby," I say out loud, "he's gone again," and I can't help but smile.

I phone the office and explain why I haven't been in, and they seem happy with my excuse of car trouble. The rest of the day is gone all too quickly. I do the dishes and put some washing on, then clean the bathroom and change my bedclothes – they still smell of him and it will keep me awake if I don't change them.

Evening falls, and I have a drink and listen to some music on the tv. Later, slipping into a fresh clean bed, I think about what happened last night and all the emotions come flooding back. Did it really happen: the car, the shower? Did he stay? Why the hell does someone so good looking want me? Shit! I sit up in bed and think, 'How the hell am I going to get to work tomorrow? I don't have a car. Crap, shit, bollocks!'

I search downstairs for my phone in my bag and yep, it's dead. I hope the girls haven't tried to call me. I plug my phone into the charger next to my bed and wait for it to fire up; it takes forever, and I'm so tired I fall asleep waiting for it. My alarm wakes me at seven, I roll over and look at my phone: there is a message from Simon. My heart leaps when I read it: 'Good morning, sleepy head. I made the decision to have a hire car delivered to your door so you can get to work. PS don't be late,' and I can't help but smile and jump out of bed, and there outside my front door sits a shiny blue Ford Focus ST, and I'm floored.

"What the hell!" I scream, and I text him back and say, 'Thank you, but I would have caught the bus.' It's a lie – I hate the bus. I don't get a reply and that kind of makes me sad, but I'm so excited, I can't wait to get dressed. He amazes me at every turn.

CHAPTER FOURTEEN

I'm dressed in my black skirt, with my pale pink sweater hanging off my shoulders, and I feel sexy. I've eaten and brushed my teeth; so, heading to the door, I see the keys to the car on the door mat and I do a silly little dance. Leaving the house, I close the door behind me. The Focus is stunning; I mean, it's a sexy car. I climb in and start the engine. Whoa, I smile, gripping the steering wheel, this sounds amazing, and I can tell it's brand new.

I connect my phone to the stereo and hit playlist shuffle: Pia Mia sings 'Do It Again', so I turn it up, and I start singing as I pull out of my street. I feel like a teenager who's got her first kiss, and I know it's only a loan, but, my god, I love it! It's beautiful to drive, and getting onto the main road, I put my foot down. 'Wow, she really moves,' I giggle.

When I pull up at work and park in the car park, locking my new toy, I wonder how much longer I will have her. I must ask Simon today after the meeting. As I walk in, I can't help but feel this place seems more like home to me than my actual home at the minute. I miss the girls already, but when they get back I will have so much to tell them.

Miles is just in front of me as I head in, Cecile is making coffee and Mervin is coming out of the toilet – he spends every morning in there doing god knows what, which makes me cringe. Celina comes from Simon's office and says good morning. I contemplate going in there as well this morning: I need to see him and see how things lie between us. I say good morning back as I head for the kitchen, grabbing a tea-bag from the drawer and placing it in the tea compartment of the coffee machine. I then grab a mug, as Celina leans on the worktop with her arms folded in front of her; she looks so elegant – like, all the damn time, and it's sickening.

"How was your weekend?" she says, and I think I see a hint of, 'Come on then, tell me all about it' in her face.

I smile while waiting for the hot water to finish its cycle and say, "Oh, you know, the usual, laundry and cleaning. I even changed my bedclothes." Okay, Ruby, stop now, she doesn't need to hear that boring shit.

Celina sighs and says, "I know what you mean: nothing exciting ever seems to happen to me. My life is probably just as dull as yours." She sighs again, and I can't help but think, thanks, Celina, for saying my life is dull, even though is isn't.

Well, it isn't at the moment and I can't help but think to myself, 'Thank your lucky stars you're not me, love.' I smile a bright smile and say, "Yeah, I know what you mean."

"I just wish some knight in shining armour would sweep me off my feet," she says.

I stir my tea and look at her. "Celina," I say, "if you like Miles then tell him you like him. Just go for it – what have you got to lose?"

She laughs and screws up her nose. "No, Ruby, I don't think so; he's not the one for me, he's not the one I'm interested in."

I say "Sorry, I didn't know you had your eye on anyone else." Then I think, 'Oh god, I hope she's not meaning Mervin'; that is a thought that makes me almost throw my tea back up!

"I mean, he never shows an interest," she adds, and this is lost on me because she's beautiful, and why wouldn't he be interested, whoever he is? But before I can ask her about this mystery man, she jumps up and says, "Oh, I have to go," just as Simon comes from the other room, wearing a smart grey suit, looking all sexy and dominant. He slings his jacket over his shoulders and I'm not sure if he's aware I'm here watching him like a lion watching its prey, but as he walks out the door and turns to close it, he locks eyes with me and gives me an all-teeth gleaming smile, and I think I felt my heart melt out of my body. I smile back and he closes the door.

This man has got me good; I think I've lost the plot, and my inner goddess is dancing around, shaking her booty.

I have a good catch-up with Cecile about her new man and she tells me he's moving in. "Wow," I say. "I'm in shock – you only met him a few weeks ago," but I realise I seem really bitter when I say it.

She smiles and says, "Well, yes, I know it seems soon, but we have fallen in love and, well, I want to be with him, and he makes me feel young again, like a child with a new toy," she adds.

I feel guilty for saying it: why shouldn't she be happy at her age? "Of course," I say. "Yes, you have every right to be happy. Don't listen to me, I'm just bitter and twisted!" I laugh.

She relaxes in her chair and says, "Well, you seem to have a bit of attention yourself, I see," and I instantly know she means Simon.

I feel really awkward, but don't show it. I just smile and say, "Well, shall we get on with some organising?"

We spend the rest of the day chatting about the launch party: we have a couple of media celebrities and a couple of high-end models on the guest list, but nothing has been confirmed yet; and a few more down-to-earth not so celebrity people – the main guests are mainly our biggest distributors. The venue is none other than the spa and hotel I stayed at, and when this was announced by Simon with a big smile on his face, I couldn't help but think of my weekend there, and this made me chuckle on the inside. I wonder if they got that stain out of the stairwell carpet?

We have hired their entire function room with its own private bar, and what a room it is – or so Celina tells me, as she's the one who went to speak with the manager and had a tour and has done the negotiations. She couldn't wait to tell me all about it! We have the hotel caterers putting together an extensive menu and a fully stocked bar, which pleases me the most. With Simon and Jonathan being the guest speakers, it will be a very elegant event; plus, we all get to stay the night, so I can drink as much as I like, and I'm thinking me and Simon could recreate the stairwell scenario, and this makes me very happy.

So, when Friday's meeting comes around and I'm asked to attend, which I've done for the past few weeks, I can't help but feel nervous. I don't like meetings, I don't like speaking; I just want to be in the background where nobody sees me. Simon has been in and out of the office all week, so I have hardly seen him; but he did email me, telling me the blue car was mine for the time being as my trusted Escort was kind of shagged. Oh, I like that word! Okay, well I need to sort a new car then: I don't want to owe him anything. So much for popping in to see him whenever I feel like it. I get it this is a busy time, and this is a big deal, and to top it all off I've not had one message apart from the email, or phone call or house call from him all week. I can't help but wonder if last weekend was just a dream – but then I look outside and my shiny blue car still sits in the car park and this pleases me. He sure is a complicated man.

In the meeting, they all think it's a good idea for me to do a presentation to introduce the new line and tell everyone how this line came to be. I look at Simon and plead silently that I don't want to do it, that I can't do it and I'm scared shitless. He must be able to see my pain, my begging, please don't make me, but he just smiles and cocks his head to one side as if confused.

The meeting wraps up at four thirty and everyone starts packing up, ready to go home. The office is busy and people are chatting loudly about the launch party next week, and what people will wear. The boys are taking the piss out of each other, saying that Mervin should wear a dress and that Miles should go in his birthday suit. This makes everyone laugh. Cecile wants me to go with her to the hotel on Monday so we can look at the menu one more time and finalise the choices, making sure we have covered all allergies and so on. This will be the first time going back since Simon showed up and so savagely took me on the stairs.

With everyone left or nearly left, me and Simon are the only ones sitting at the table. He is opposite me and he looks so good: his hair has grown and I can't help but think it makes him look so much younger than his thirty-five years.

"Well," he finally says, "what do you think?" and

he gives me a smile.

"What do I think?" I say. "I am shell-shocked, Simon. I can't speak in front of all those people; I will just be a babbling mess. I will say the wrong thing and everyone will laugh at me. I feel like crying," I add.

He rises from his chair and walks around the table towards me – god, he's hot! He takes a seat next to me and crosses his legs and rests his weight on the arm of the chair so his body is half-facing me, and with a big smile he says, "What are you afraid of? What do you think could possibly happen to you?" he adds. "I will be up there with you, as will Jonathan?" Ah, yes, the infamous Jonathan who I've never actually met but have only heard his voice over the speaker-phone in one of our many meetings. He's worse than Simon for not showing up.

I turn to Simon and I reply, "What if everyone laughs at me or they think I'm a big fat joke and boo me off stage?" I say with a low, sad voice.

"Ruby Frankton, you are not a joke. You have some super great ideas and I think people need to hear how this all came to be, how this line all started – and you're one of the most beautiful people I've ever had the pleasure of knowing, and I'm so glad I hired you; and if they boo you, then they will have me to deal with."

I look at him wide-eyed and full of wonder and lust and shock all at the same time. He just called me beautiful. "Look," he says, "how about we discuss it further when I come see you later."

"Later?" I say. When was this discussed? Fuck, yes, I want to see him later, I think, my head in turmoil. Can we have a normal evening together that doesn't involve chasing each other and him being dominant? I mean, yes, okay, that's great, but he cannot just keep turning up and not give me warning he's coming. I tell him I need to go see Cecile before she goes, but it's a lie; I just need to leave his presence because he's fucking hot and I want to fuck him on the table.

He nods in agreement, and we stand at the same time. He smiles with his hands placed in his pockets and says, "Is nine o'clock okay, or is that too late?"

I look at him, stepping forward so I am close to him, but not too close. I can smell his delicious aftershave and I know he wants to touch me. I say, "Yes, nine o'clock is fine, but we really should try and keep it professional at work," to which he laughs and steps even closer to me. I smell his messy hair and we touch foreheads, and I tell him in a low, calm voice that I love him – not because I want him to know, but because I want it to be said loud and make it clear my feelings for him are real, and that's why, when I'm at work, we need to keep our distance.

He gives a deep sigh and replies, "I know you do. I've known for a while, and when you told me the other day in a roundabout way…" He sighs again and he speaks with a clear voice. "You know that I care for you deeply, Ruby."

His words bore into my soul. "Yes," I reply, but I lie. I've never known how he feels, I've never known exactly where I stand. He is so conflicting, I just don't know what to think half the bloody time. I tell him I need to go, at which he stands back while I gather my papers and leave the room, feeling lost. 'Great,' I think, 'he cares and I truly believe he cares a lot; but I love him and I'm not sure him caring is enough for me, but then maybe it is. Oh god, I need a drink.' I head out to the kitchen and see Cecile just as she's walking out of the door, 'Bye' she calls as she shuts the door. I say 'bye' back and gather my bag and jacket, heading to my car. I turn to the office and see Simon looking at me through his office window. I can tell his hands are in his pockets and I know he's in turmoil over us – he's not accustomed to love and feelings. Well, I am, and I'm not afraid to show it. I climb in my for-now new car and shut the door, take out my phone and choose a song for my journey home: Selena Gomez's 'Good For You' seems to be a good song.

CHAPTER FIFTEEN

I start the car with a roar and pull out of the car park, fully aware Simon is still watching me. I speed along the A47, going well over the speed limit, but I don't care – this car deserves to be driven fast. The roads are dry and the sun has just started going down.

Parking outside my house, I contemplate not going in and not being home when he calls. Maybe I should just keep driving until I run out of petrol, then he would have to rescue me again. 'Yeah, good one, Ruby,' I say in my head in a child-like voice.

Eventually, I head indoors, and as I shut my front door I can't help but miss my girls. They will be back next Sunday, and I'm quite sad I'm not picking them up from the airport: Jessica's friend's mum is collecting them all – and because of my launch night Saturday, they didn't want me to drive Sunday with a hangover. This thought makes me smile.

Walking into the kitchen, I grab the vodka from the freezer and pour a large glass, adding only a small amount of Coke. The first mouthful makes me inhale sharply, then I head upstairs for a shower; it's just past five-thirty, so I have time to shower, eat and make myself look pretty for when he arrives. I'm so nervous and I don't know why; maybe it's because it's planned and it feels like a date, almost. 'Okay, Ruby, just calm yourself and let's see how the night pans out.'

Climbing in the shower, I'm suddenly filled with emotions of that night I lost the plot – this shower brings good and bad memories flooding back. I shave my legs and trim my more delicate areas. I then wash my hair, and, once satisfied, I turn off the water and climb out of the shower. I dry myself and walk naked to my bedroom, where I pick out my best thong and matching bra. It feels like it's my first time, like it's my first ever date and I want it to be right. I go through my closet, picking a sexy but casual outfit: I decide on some black shorts and a white slim-fitting vest. Yes, I think when I look in the mirror, my boobs look good and I feel slim. This will do, I say, as I finish the rest of my drink.

I head downstairs to make some food, pouring myself another vodka. I need to eat something light, so I make myself some toast. I choose some music and settle on the sofa. He will be here soon, and my stomach is in knots. Why does he make me feel this way?

Nine o'clock comes and goes. I keep looking at my phone, but I get nothing to say he's running late or he's not coming, so I just presume he will be here when he gets here. Ten o'clock comes and goes. I feel brave and a little pissed off, so I send him a message asking if he's okay. I get no reply and now I'm getting concerned. I message him again thirty minutes later, asking if he's in trouble or if he's had an accident, but I get no reply. 'This is nuts!' I yell at my phone.

By eleven o'clock I've drunk half a bottle of vodka and I've gotten more angry as the time's gone by. How dare he fucking ignore me! How dare he make me feel this way yet again!

By midnight I'm so drunk I'm sitting on my living room floor, singing sad love songs. I've not heard a thing and I'm heartbroken. I really thought we had turned a corner. He seemed so sincere today, but I guess I was wrong. By one in the morning I climb the stairs one by one, in the hope that every step will swallow me whole and I won't have to face the world again tomorrow. I sink into my bed and pass out, and I have a very disturbed sleep. I wake several times when I see lights outside, thinking it could be him finally turning up, but it never is, and I soon fall asleep again.

Saturday morning and my head feels like I've been hit by a train. I stumble downstairs and get a glass of water and take it back upstairs to my bed. I feel so sick, and I know it's self-inflicted, but I fall asleep again. Waking at 2pm, I check my phone and I have a message from the girls, asking if I'm okay and to say they are having a fab time. I can't help but smile; at least they are having a good holiday. I don't see any other messages, so I decide to get up and have a shower. I wash my hair and brush my teeth, then cry for a few minutes and bang the wall in frustration. 'That's it,' I tell myself, 'no more! I can't do this any more; I need to put a stop to it and fast.'

I waste the day on the sofa. I've eaten all sorts of weird and wonderful combinations, and I've watched three movies. Sunday is pretty much the same. It's like the world has stopped, but I'm still moving. I'm on auto-pilot. I crank up the music and sing along to Rihanna's 'Stay'. I can't help but look out of the window every time I hear a noise. The weather looks lovely, but I don't want to go out. I'm just glad the girls aren't here to see this – they would definitely be giving him a piece of their mind; but I just think, when all is said and done, I should just walk away. I want to get the launch party done and dusted, and only then can I leave with my head held high.

Monday comes all too soon and I'm dressed in my best black skinny jeans and a soft white t-shirt. My hair is down and my make-up is on point. I look in the hall mirror and I put on a smile, chanting to myself to be strong and tell him it's over, but my heart aches: I don't want it to be over

I climb in my for-now car and hit the open carriageway. The roads are quiet and the sun is bright and warm. Mika sings about a happy ending, and I can't help but think there will be no happy ending for me. Parking at work, I can instantly see Simon's car is not there and that tells me he's taken himself off again for a few days; typical Simon – can't commit. I walk in and see Cecile by the coffee machine. We say our good mornings and arrange to leave for the hotel at ten sharp. As I pour the milk into my tea that I collected on the way in, Celina breezes in, and she looks stunning as usual. She joins us at the coffee machine and announces that Simon is out of town for the rest of the week. 'Wait, what?' I'm screaming in my head. 'Out of town! Why?'

"He's had some personal issues to deal with," she adds, telling us that she will be stepping in to deal with any problems that may arise in his absence.

Cecile looks at me and gives a concerned look. She takes her coffee and joins Miles in the other room just as Mervin exits the toilet. Celina gives me a very wide smile and makes herself a coffee. "So," she finally says, "are you and Cecile all set for today's final walk-round?"

I can't focus. I can't stop thinking about Simon having personal issues. "Hello, earth to Ruby!" She snaps her fingers and laughs.

I look at her wide-eyed and say, "Sorry, yes, we are ready for the final walk-round.

"Good." She smiles. "Well, you know where I am if you need me," and with that, she grabs her coffee and walks off in the direction of Simon's office.

I must have stood in the kitchen for a long time as the tea I had made was nearly cold. 'Oh god, where is he?' I wonder. 'I hope he's okay.'

It's nine o'clock and Cecile and I are on the road, heading for the hotel. We use my car because, well, it's nicer than Cecile's. We arrive at the hotel and park close to reception, and, as I climb out of the car, it brings back so many memories. I smile and take a deep breath as I lock the car and we head inside. The reception is just the same. 'Well, of course it is!' I yell in my head. 'It was only a couple of weeks ago, you idiot!'

Thomas is there behind the desk and I'm so surprised when he looks up and greets me with, "Good morning, Ms Frankton, welcome back."

"Good morning, Thomas," I say with a smile. "We are here to see Mr Stanley for a final walk-round."

He gives us a never-ending smile and nods, picks up the phone and speaks clearly. "Mr Stanley, your 10.30 appointment is here." He then nods and says, "Very good, sir." Wow, how formal, I think. He replaces the phone and looks back at us. "Mr Stanley will be out shortly," he says. "Can I offer you ladies a hot beverage?" he adds.

I smile and say, "No, thank you." Cecile says the same, so he comes around the desk and asks us to proceed to the bar area to have a seat at one of the empty tables, which we do. There is a lovely smell of coffee in the air, and there are cleaners rushing around, clearing up after the breakfast service.

Mr Stanley walks in with large, wide steps and

talks quite loud, saying, "Good morning, ladies; please, shall we head to the kitchen to see chef?" He looks in a hurry, but I'm sure he's just a busy man. He shakes both our hands and we follow him around the back of the bar to the right and into a large well-stocked kitchen. It's very clean and there are people all in white, busy preparing food, probably for the lunch menu. Potatoes are all over the counter, ready to be chopped, and there are what looks like fruit on sticks. We meet the head chef and he confirms the entrées of rockmelon bruschetta with goats' cheese and prosciutto, crispy bocconcini with tomato chilli sauce, and finally a grilled seafood platter. It sounds amazing. I look at Cecile and raise my eyebrows as if to say wow, and she smiles back in excitement.

The chef looks at us both and says, "Are you happy with that?"

We both nod and say, "Absolutely."

"Okay, good," he says. "So, when the show has concluded, we will have everyone seated and we will bring out mustard stuffed chicken, oven-baked lamb risotto and, for the vegetarians, a one-pot mushroom and potato curry."

I can feel my mouth watering. "That sounds super yummy," I say.

The chef smiles at me and says, "I need a final list of allergies no later than Thursday."

I reply, "That's absolutely fine."

Cecile then asks Mr Stanley if we can see the

final room layout, to which he says, "Of course."

The chef nods and walks away; we then leave the kitchen and head to the main function room. Celina is right: it's stunning, with its high ceiling and huge chandelier. They have spaced out twenty-five round tables, all with white tablecloths, and each with ten blue chairs with shiny gold mouldings pushed beneath them. To the left is a raised stage with stairs to the right, and a navy blue curtain hanging down the back, held up by a huge gold curtain pole with intricate gold carvings. It looks spectacular. Mr Stanley tells us he is planning to have lights across the back of the stage to make it sparkle more, and when he says this I smile, because I can tell he's just as excited as we are. "And we also plan on having a walkway come out of the stage at the front so people can see the models more clearly when sitting around the edge," he adds. "There will be chairs on both sides of the stage, so everyone will have a good view of the show."

"Well," says Cecile, "I'm impressed. You certainly have thought of everything."

Mr Stanley offers a broad smile, and we then ask if we can have a few more minutes to walk around, and, of course, he obliges. "If I can help you with anything else, please do not hesitate to call me."

We say our thank you and tell him he's been very kind, and he then excuses himself and leaves. Cecile walks up to the stage and says, "Wow, Ruby, I don't envy you standing up there!"

I look at her and shake my head. "Please don't," I say. "I feel sick thinking about it."

Happy with all we have seen, we head back to the car, saying goodbye to Thomas on the way. I call back to him and say, "See you Saturday," to which he gives a little wave.

Back at the office, we all gather together to have a quick chat about the food and the layout. Everyone is buzzing and excited. "This is one of the biggest advertisements we have ever done," says Mervin.

So Miles pipes up and says, "Yeah, but it's not as big as your mum's knickers!" We all laugh, with Mervin flipping him the birdie.

Celina calms everyone down and says in her very elegant voice, "Guys, this is going to be fantastic, and I want you all looking your best, so it's been cleared with Mr Boon for you all to have Friday afternoon off so you can all go and get pampered and preened." She smiles.

'Wow,' I think, 'how generous!' It's been lovely not seeing Simon; I really don't think I could have dealt with him and the hotel in one day, but I do miss him and wonder if he's okay. Celina has done a great job; she's calm and positive, keeping up the team's morale.

The rest of the week goes by slowly, but that's always the case when you have something to look forward to. When Friday morning comes, everyone is in fine spirits. I need to go pick up my black dress from the dry cleaners; it's not been worn since I don't know when, but I tried it on and it looks damn good. It's floor-length in soft satin with cascading ruffles and it's backless. I just hope I don't get hot up on the stage, as I don't want people to see my sweaty under-arms. I cringe.

Cecile tells me she's gone for a pale blue A-line V-neck evening dress, floor-length, with a split front, and I can't help but think she's brave; but I'm sure she will look beautiful.

We have a team meeting to arrange what jobs are to be done on Saturday morning and who is to oversee what. Myself and Celina are in charge of making sure the tables are all arranged and every guest has a goodie bag, which contains a silk scarf for the ladies, ballpoint pen set and a mini water bottle, aftershave for the men and hair scrunchies for the women. They also get a mini bottle of champagne. It's all very cool and I wish I was getting one. Cecile is in charge of the catwalk models: she has to organise when they come on and in what order. Miles is in charge of the music and lighting effects. Well, I say he's in charge. I mean he's in charge of making sure the DJ follows our set; Miles will be lingering around the bar area. I'm not jealous at all. He will make sure everyone has a drink and is happy; I'm still not convinced he's the best man for the job, but he sounds confident when he speaks about it.

We all pack up at one o'clock and have a general chit-chat about the upcoming event. Miles asks Celina if the boss man will be there, and all eyes are on Celina. She smiles and says. "I'm sure he will make every effort to be there," and my heart skips a beat. Okay, so he may be there. I think I'm going to be sick.

We all head out to the car park and Cecile locks the door. "See you tomorrow, everyone."

"Yes," says Mervin, "I'll be the one naked and drunk at the bar."

Miles shouts out, "That's disgusting!"

So Mervin replies, "That's not what your mum said this morning."

I giggle and shake my head.

CHAPTER SIXTEEN

I drive into town and collect my dress, carefully hanging it in the back of my car. I then head to the hair salon for my two o'clock appointment for a colour and a trim. Tracey is my stylist for the afternoon and she's probably early forties, like me. She's overweight, but then so am I. She chats with everyone else in the room bar me, and when she's finally done, she doesn't even look at me when I pay. I won't be going there again, but I must say I love it – she's done a great job. There's not many times I come out of a salon and say that.

Back at home, I eat a grilled cheese sandwich and pack my case, drinking vodka and listening to Justin Bieber. How sad is my life? I get a text from the girls wishing me good luck and that they are so proud of me. I tell them I miss them and I can't wait to see them Sunday night, and they tell me they want plenty of pictures and all the hot gossip. I laugh and tell them it's not that sort of event.

I climb into bed and it's just after ten o'clock. I must be mad or bloody tired, because I'm soon asleep. I dream of Simon: he tells everyone in the room I'm his lady and that he loves me; then I'm pregnant and he's holding my belly, looking at me with that smile; then he's gone and I'm by the sea. I wake up staring at the ceiling. Wow, what a vivid dream! I feel my stomach and smile, Simon's words coming back like a boomerang: he doesn't think he wants kids. Well, I must say I don't want any more because I'm too old; well, I class myself as too old, but I would consider it for him. I've not really thought of him all week, and yet here I am dreaming of him. I get up and dress in casual jeans and white pumps, with my soft pink hoody, and I leave the house at nine on the dot, checking all things are turned off, and, hanging my dress in the back of my for-now car, I drive the scenic route to the hotel. The sun is shining and the traffic is light. I still feel flutters in my stomach about tonight and the thought he may be there. I pull into the long gravel drive and past the raised flower beds and park my car. Celina has just about vanished inside, and I can see Miles climbing out of the front of Cecile's car. 'Oh, how sweet,' I think, 'she gave him a lift'; but no sign of Mervin – he's probably in the bathroom, like I swear he always is.

We greet each other with a good morning and head in together, me pulling my case behind me. We go to the main desk area, where Celina has already checked us in. I'm sure Thomas would have been in a fluster when she walked in, because even in her casual clothes she looks beautiful. I lock eyes with Thomas and he says, "Hello, good to see you again,

Ms Frankton." He's always smiling.

The hotel is alive with activity: people cleaning, moving stuff out, bringing stuff in, even a red carpet rolled out at the entrance – it really does feel like Hollywood. My room is on the third floor, room 78, and I'm disappointed I didn't have the same room as last time. Celina tells everyone to go settle in and come down for a brief meeting in one hour, to which we all smile and start chatting as we head for the elevator. It's only when I'm standing in front it that I see my reflection in the shiny gold door, and a vision of Simon standing behind me pops into my head, which makes me smile. The door opens and we all climb in, and, with the doors closing, Mervin whispers something to Miles and he tries to hide a giggle. There is a ping to announce the second floor, at which Miles and Mervin get out, with Mervin calling "See you later, ladies."

I can't help but smile and say, "Not if we see you first!" The doors close and we are all quiet. It must be nerves, or the fact that, with no boys to entertain us, we are, in fact, boring. We arrive on the third floor, where myself and Celina head right with Cecile heading left. Again, we call "See you soon" to each other. Celina stops at room 70 and I'm glad it's not room 69, which is a room I hold dear to me.

In my new room, I have the same layout as before. Everything now reminds me of that night, and I know I need to walk the stairs at some point. I walk over to the window and look out at the lawns. It really is beautiful here: it's calm and serene. I unpack my suitcase and suddenly remember I've left my dress in the car. Shit, bollocks! Now I have to go all the way down to my car to get it. How could I forget such a thing?

I leave my case and decide to head down and retrieve it. I lean on the wall, waiting for the elevator to arrive, watching the number 2 come and go, and with a ping the door slides open and out steps Simon, who now stands right before me. Oh my fucking god! I'm stunned. He's fucking here, and I don't know what to do. He gives me that sexy smile and says in a very apologetic way, "Miss me?"

I can't speak. My face must say it all. What the fuck? I press the button again as the door has shut – I need to go get my dress – then the door opens again and I step inside. He spins around with his hands in his pockets, and he's still smiling as the doors close. I fall back against the wall of the elevator. I don't want to deal with his bullshit – I can't deal with his bullshit. Not today.

I walk to my for-now car and unlock it, grab my dress from the back and lock the car again. My legs like jelly, I head back inside. I see Thomas standing at reception. He smiles and I think he can see the look of dread on my face, because he steps out from around the desk and asks me if I'm okay.

"No, Thomas, I'm not," I say. "I'm not okay. I

need a stiff drink," I add.

"Oh, honey," he says, "follow me." He leads me through the dining area that used to have tables in but is now quite clear, straight to the bar, and we go to the far end and he grabs the vodka and pours me a large measure with a small amount of Coke, handing it to me. I take it with shaking hands and down it, then shake my head when I'm done. He looks at me with an open mouth and says, "Wow, you needed that!"

"Yes, Thomas," I say with a screwed-up shit that was strong face, "I absolutely did." He pours me another and hands it to me, but I decide not to down this one as I can't get drunk before the party – I would be fired for sure. Thomas just waits patiently for me to speak, and I then explain the whole fucked-up thing with Simon and that he's playing with me and I'm letting him get away with it. Thomas just smiles and nods; he's a very good listener. I ask him what I should do. "I've only known him a couple of months and I'm in love with him, but he doesn't love me."

Before I know it, an hour has passed and Celina walks elegantly into the bar area, wearing tight-cropped black trousers and a white ruffle sleeveless blouse and killer heels. I don't know how she does it. I smile at Thomas and he says, "Honey, in god we trust," and I look at him, puzzled. He smiles and continues, "Look, what will be will be; just let it happen. Why worry over something you can't control?" He squeezes my hand as he leaves.

Cecile soon arrives, while Miles and Mervin are laughing as they enter the room. We all gather at a small round table. I'm still holding my drink and my dress is draped over my arm, and Miles looks at me like, 'Whoa, it's like eleven in the morning'. I give him a look of 'Fuck off, I'll drink when I damn well want and what I damn well want'; but just then I hear his voice – that sexy bastard has come to join us. Simon walks in all casual, speaking with everyone. He says sorry for his absence and for Celina to carry on, and she smiles at him with a twinkle in her eye; but he's looking straight at me. He grabs a chair and spins it around so when he sits astride it his arms are resting on the back. He is right next to me, and I can feel his heat and I can smell his smell. I shuffle in my chair, trying to get it to move, and drink my drink. Celina thanks us all for coming early on a Saturday morning. We are all super-excited for the evening events; we did have a lot to organise, but with the thirty extra staff that have been brought in, it should run smoothly. "I've given Mr Stanley the itinerary for tonight and it's taken a lot of heat off our shoulders. I would still like to see you all on your best behavior." She looks at the boys when she says it, to which they look at each other in shock messing about. "I want everyone to have fun, enjoy the night, enjoy the food, and enjoy the show." She then goes on to talk about the drinks and the food. "Please keep an eye on everyone to make sure they don't choke or that they haven't been ignored." Finally, she says with a smile, "Nine o'clock sharp, Ruby will say her speech."

I splutter, almost choking on my drink. "Speech?" I say, looking around. "No, I'm just saying a few words; that's it." I look straight at Simon, who is still fucking smiling.

"Okay, well, we can discuss this later," she says.

I smile and think, 'Yeah, we can, but I'm probably going to be drunk by then, and I'm still not doing a fucking speech!'

With everyone happy about the day ahead, I leave my dress on the chair as we all head into the giant hall to see the finished look. The tables are laid beautifully, the glasses all shine and sparkle, there are tiny crystals spread over the tablecloth and there are name tags on the plates where people will sit. I wander around, trying to find my seat, and I'm relieved I'm next to Cecile, but also shocked when I see I'm sitting next to Mr Boon. I'm aware Simon is right behind me, but I don't turn; instead, I walk over to the stage and I can't help but feel sick.

Simon stands beside me and says, "You will be fine. I'll be there with you." He's smiling again. What the fuck is it with him smiling?

I turn and say quietly, "Okay, so you will be right next to me, like you have been for the last week, yeah?" I shake my head in disappointment and I walk away. I go to speak with Cecile and tell her we are sitting next to each other, and when I turn around,

Simon is speaking with Celina and she has her hand on his arm. This pisses me off, because he allows her to touch him but I never was; what a fucking joke. I tell Cecile I'm going to the bar and I walk out of the room.

I get to the bar and put down my now empty glass and I see Simon coming through the doorway, so I make a hasty retreat out into the lobby and down the long corridor to the swimming pool. I instantly know he's behind me and I run in the hope I can hide from him. As I dart into the ladies' toilet and slam the door behind me, I try to catch my breath. He won't come in here, surely? But no, I am wrong: he bursts open the door and lunges towards me. I try to reach for the door to leave, but he grabs my hand and he holds my wrist behind my back so I am pressed up against him. He spins me to the left so I end up with my back against one of the toilet doors. "Don't you fucking dare!" I yell. "I mean it – I will fucking scream."

He smiles and yanks my jeans undone, saying, "No you won't, Ruby, because you want me to fuck you, and I'm going to fuck you hard and fast." He pushes me back so we are now in the toilet stall, and the door slams shut behind him.

"Simon, I mean it! This isn't fair – you can't keep doing this to me." He kisses my neck and grabs my breasts from underneath my hoody. I try to push him off, but he's too strong for me.

He looks at me so we are face to face. "Tell me to

leave," he says, all hot. I am breathing hard, but I don't want him to leave. I can't say it, I can't say a word. "Tell me to fucking leave, Ruby!" he snarls at me, and I know I can't. He kisses me hard, all lips and tongues and arms; he yanks my jeans down and I take one shoe off and pull one leg out. He has reached under my hoody again and undone my bra so he can cup my bare breasts and he twists my hard nipples. He is kissing my neck and I'm silently begging for his tongue on my clit. He lifts my right leg up on the toilet seat and he yanks open his own trousers; he then drops to his knees so his head is level with my pussy, and he wastes no time as he plunges his tongue deep inside my soft wet folds. I grab his hair and pull hard; I pull him in. He grabs my buttocks with his hands and I drop my head back and call out 'fuck' over and over again. He's flicking my clit again and again, with his soft tongue sending me over the edge. I can't hold it, it's too good, so I come hard and fast, like my body needed it, needed him. He doesn't wait for my trembling to stop; he stands and in one swift move his cock penetrates me, and he rams into me with a new urgency, like I am his drug and he needs a fix. Our growls and moans blend into one, as harder and harder he moves, and I cling to his shoulders until he fills me once more and lets go. He, too, comes hard, yelling my name over and over, and then slows to a stop, breathing heavily into my neck.

This man is my enemy, yet I can't help but want

him, and I know now he wants me, too – he must do, or he wouldn't be here now, doing what he's doing. He pulls out and steps back and I quickly lift the toilet seat and sit down – I don't want a sticky mess running down my leg. He stands back some more and pulls up his trousers, tucking in his white shirt; then runs his hands through his newly cut hair, and my god, he's a vision.

I wipe myself and pull up my thong and jeans. Slipping on my shoe, I stand to meet him, clipping my bra back up. "What the fuck, Simon?" I say.

He leans on the door and says, "Sorry."

"Sorry?" I yell. "Where have you been? I've been worried sick. I messaged you, no reply; I messaged you again, but no fucking reply; then Celina steps in."

"Okay, okay." He holds up his hands. "Sorry, I'm a selfish prick, I know." He looks at the floor and back at me with tired eyes. "Ruby, my father died."

I stare at him. Shit, shit, shit! I have no words, I am stunned.

"I have been arranging his funeral and I had to take care of my mother."

"Simon, I'm so sorry. I…I'm sorry, I don't know what to say. How? I mean, are you okay?"

"Yes, I am now." He smiles. "My father had Alzheimer's and was in a care home. He developed cancer of the liver; it was all very quick."

I stand with my hands on my hips, looking at this broken man standing before me. "Simon," I say, but just then the door opens and we hear what sounds like the cleaner pulling in a cart. Oh, shit!

He smiles, moving forward so we are once again close; he kisses me softly, holding my face, and I melt into his hands. After a few minutes, the cleaner leaves and we exit the toilet. "Simon," I say, "we can't keep doing this; you can't keep doing this to me – it's not fair."

He looks at the floor and puts his hands in his pockets. "I know," he finally says. "I know you deserve more and maybe we can discuss it later, after the party," he adds.

Okay, I nod with half a smile, because I know I will be too drunk and he will probably disappear again; but I will remain hopeful. We walk back up the main corridor to reception and he briefly holds my hand; this makes my heart do somersaults, and I see Thomas give me a cheeky smile. He holds up my dress with a thumbs-up, and I smile back, nodding my head as if to say thank you for looking after it.

CHAPTER SEVENTEEN

We join the others in the hall just as Celina announces she is off for a swim, which everyone agrees is a fantastic idea. "Will you be joining us, Simon?" she adds.

"Unfortunately not," he says, making his excuses and telling us that he will see us all down here ready to go at six o'clock. He looks at me as if to say 'Sorry, I need to sort some stuff', then he's gone again. I smile because I don't want the others to see that there's anything between us, and my heart is fit to burst, and I smile because of what we just did a few moments ago.

We all head back through the lobby and upstairs. I grab my dress from Thomas as I go past, saying thank you, and thirty minutes later we all rejoin in the pool area. Celina is already in the pool doing laps; Mervin and Miles are in the jacuzzi, laughing about something; and Cecile is sitting on the edge of the pool with her feet dipped in. She has some shorts on over her swimsuit as if to hide a million sins. I find an empty lounger and take off my shoes, then pull off my jeans. Slipping my hoody over my head and tossing it on the lounger, I dive into the pool. I'm so glad I got rid of the other swimsuit and opted for a plain black one. I swim to the other side and back, and the water feels so good on my skin. I rest on the wall next to Cecile and we chat about her man, and how good things are. I really am happy for her, and I'm happy she feels the need to share it with me; it feels good to have a friend again.

She looks down at me and says, "So what was all that about earlier?"

I look at her wide-eyed, as if to say 'Oh, shit, she knows.' "I don't know what you mean," I say with a funny face, but she looks at me with 'don't bullshit me' eyes. "Cecile, honestly, I don't know what you mean." There was no moment earlier and even if there was, I would not feel comfortable telling anyone.

"Okay," says Cecile, "that's fine if you don't want to talk about it, but just know I'm here, okay?"

I just look at her and smile. No, I don't want to talk about it; and with that, I swim another four lengths of the pool. Celina climbs out of the pool and up the metal steps, looking stunning in her bikini – of course she does: she's got a cracking figure. She walks to the jacuzzi and climbs in with the boys. She has a certain confidence I wish I had.

Cecile gets up off the side and walks over to a lounger, grabbing her things as she waves at me and leaves the pool room; it's obviously not her thing. I climb out of the water and lay on one of the loungers. I feel drained; I have so many emotions running through my head, yet again Simon being one big emotion. I towel-dry my hair and then lay back to relax.

Celina gets out of the jacuzzi and comes to lay on the lounger next to me. With a big sigh, she turns to me and smiles. "Is everything all right?" I ask her.

"Ruby, I think tonight could be the night to tell him how I feel."

I turn to her and say, "Who is this mystery man, Celina?"

She smiles and says, "You will all find out soon enough."

"I really would love to know," I say again.

She sits up and spins her long legs around to face me, and in a quiet voice she says, "Okay, it's Mr Hails." She gives me a huge smile and claps her hands together.

My heart is in my mouth, and the look on my face must have said it all. "Oh, wow," I say in a shocked voice. "How long have you been into him?" I cough.

"Only since like forever. He's a dreamboat, isn't he?" she sighs.

"Um, yes, he certainly is," I reply, shaking my head.

"I'm just going to go for it and see what happens," she adds.

"Well, yes, why worry over something you can't control?" I smile at her with the sound of Thomas in my head. My brain feels like the room is spinning and

I'm thinking, 'You poor woman, you have no idea what this man is actually like; he's a headfuck for a start. Oh, and I'm fucking him!' She looks so relaxed and elegant in her baby pink bikini, all curves and tanned skin.

The boys emerge from the spa and announce they are going to the bar, at which I jump up and say, "Oh, yes, I'm in."

Celina sighs and says. "Have fun, guys – but remember, I need you all sober and up front and centre come six o'clock."

We all giggle, teasing her and saying 'yes, sir'. I pull on my jeans and slip on my hoody; I don't care that my costume is still damp – I need a drink. We get to the bar and decide to order three drinks: we all have to choose a drink for the others to down. I choose a shot of Sambuca: it burns as it goes down, but I love it. Miles picks peach schnapps, playing it safe, and Mervin orders tequila. I hate the stuff, but I drink it. We have a laugh for an hour, taking the piss out of various people who come in and out of the bar, then the boys get out their phones to show each other a funny video. I wish Simon was here. I wonder if he would drink with me. Would he laugh at silly videos? Would he do shots with me? I've never even heard him tell a joke.

Three o'clock comes all too soon and I decide to leave the boys with their heads stuck in their phones. I need a shower and to get ready for tonight, and the boys don't even look up when I leave.

Passing reception, I see Thomas. "I couldn't help but take a peek at your dress earlier," he says, "and I think you will knock him dead tonight." He flashes me a huge smile.

"I have no idea what you're talking about!" I grin back at him.

"Well, my apologies, miss, do forgive me!"

I walk away and give a little wave and he waves back. Upstairs in my room, I turn on the shower and undress. I really hope tonight goes well. I need to tell Simon about Celina – well, warn him how she feels about him. I'm feeling relaxed from the drinks; maybe I shouldn't have had so many. I really need Simon to be on his best behaviour tonight, and I really need this speech I've got floating around my head to just flow off my tongue. I don't want to make myself look foolish.

I exit the shower, dry and dress in my new underwear: it's black lace and makes me feel super-sexy. I sit in front of the mirror that hangs on the wardrobe door and do my make-up, giving myself the smokey eyes treatment – it's a very sexy look. I put my hair up on one side with a vintage diamanté and pearl hair comb, so my hair falls down over my right shoulder; and I'm wearing a diamanté crystal drop necklace that falls between my breasts; and when I finally slip on my dress over my black high-heeled sandals, I look stunning, even if I do say so myself. I don't think I even looked this good on my wedding day.

It's now six o'clock and I need to get a move on. Walking to the elevator, I wait for it to arrive to take me down to the lobby. I feel nervous and anxious, and I'm gripping my small sparkling silver clutch bag for dear life. The lift speaker announces the ground floor and the doors open, and as I step out, Cecile is the first one I see. She looks so pretty in her light blue dress, and she's smiling like a giddy teenager. She tells me I look stunning, and when I turn to my right I come face to face with Simon, looking sexy as hell, and his face is a picture of pure shock when he sees me. He mouths the word 'wow', and moves towards me, clutching my elbows and kissing my cheek.

"You look beautiful, Ruby," he whispers. "I am lost for words how stunning you are, and my god, I could fuck you right here and now," he adds, and this makes my heart do flips.

Cecile is watching us closely, and we step back just as Celina joins us from the other elevator. She is in a floor-length bright red halter-neck dress: it's backless and her hair is down all the way to the top of her buttocks. Sparkling gold sandals cradle her very pretty feet, and she looks amazing. She walks with grace and elegance, and red suits her very much. She comes up to us and goes straight for Simon, and he kisses her cheek. She lingers far longer than she needed to, and he is watching my reaction closely.

She then turns to me and Cecile and tells us we look fantastic. I tell her she looks stunning and she says, "Oh, thank you."

Simon is in a very posh-looking black suit with a black bow-tie, and he looks so sexy. It's very similar to the one he turned up in the first night he fucked me on my kitchen table, and this makes me smile, which he notices. He grabs his jacket and pulls it down tight against him, smiling back like he knows what I'm thinking. Miles and Mervin exit the elevator together, both equally handsome in their black suits, even if Miles is wearing black pumps on his feet.

"I'm so glad you boys made the effort," says Celina with a smile.

Mervin says, "Well, you could have made more of an effort yourself!" and we all laugh.

"Right, everyone, calm down," says Simon. "Let's get in there and mingle and let's have a good show." He looks at me and winks. Wow, it's like he never left. He just seems to fit back in and take up where he left off. I really need to speak with him, but there are far too many people around at the minute, so it will have to wait. I really am dreading the speech and how this night will end, but we all start to head towards the main bar area. Simon tries to hang back and walk in with me, but Celina grabs his arm and marches him off. He doesn't pull away, which kind of pisses me off; so, saying 'fuck it', I head for the bar. I don't care we have our own private bar – I just need a drink.

I pass a few people who stop me to say hello, and I get told numerous times how beautiful I look, to which I say 'thank you' lots of times. Simon is nowhere to be seen, and this again makes me feel sad. I get to the bar and order a double vodka with a dash of Coke, which I down in one, then decide to head into the main hall and find Cecile. She is talking with a woman in a shimmering long black strapless dress; she seems to be holding a tape recorder, so I guess it's someone from the local paper. I'm asked if I would like one of the entrées and I say, "No, thank you." I can't eat, not now: my stomach is in knots. I can't think: it feels like the room is spinning. I need to see where Simon is, but there are far too many people in the room. I grab a glass of champagne from one of the servers and sip it slowly. I'm not really a lover of champagne. I can see people being given their goodie bags as they enter and that makes me smile, because I see their smiles when they look inside. There are lots of people trying to find their places at the beautifully decorated round tables and lots of talk about the new line, so when seven o'clock comes around, everyone is asked to take their seats around the stage for the show to begin. I can see Cecile near the back, chatting with some of the models. God, I hope we chose wisely – we had such an influx of women wanting to show off their curves. She's there trying to organise them, even though she doesn't need to do that now.

I take a seat near the front and I'm glad when I have Mervin and Miles to my right and two *Radon* reporters to my left. I look around to see where Simon is, but I can't see him. The lights dip and the music starts: it's a Brent Faiyaz track, and it's sexy and seducing. The first model comes on with a cherry and black basque set with matching suspender belt – she looks fantastic. The lights are dipped and flashing with the music. The next model is wearing a *faux*-leather and lace corset and she looks damn good.

The next forty minutes run along smoothly. All the models seem to be a good choice and I think everyone has done an amazing job getting this whole thing up and running. Looking around at the faces of the audience, I can see they are impressed. There are lots of cameras flashing, which kind of blinds me, and I can feel the heat rising on my body for my upcoming speech. I'm still hoping for a power cut, but with the show coming to an end and all the models on the runway for a final walk, everyone stands to clap, and when the lights return to normal, we are all asked to take our seats for dinner.

So, leaving the stage area, I head to take my seat for our main meal – not that I want to eat. I place my bag under my seat as Cecile takes a seat next to me on my left. "That was amazing," she says, all heavy breathing. "It was so much better than I expected."

I smile and say, "Yes, it certainly was. You've done a great job of organising the show, and the models were just fantastic."

She then offers a big smile as a younger-looking man sits to my right and at first I don't notice him until he says, "Hello, I'm Jonathan Boon; you must be Ruby." He holds out his hand and I shake it.

"Yes," I reply, "I'm Ruby. It's a pleasure to finally meet you," I squeak.

"The pleasure is all mine," he smiles. "I've heard so much about you," he adds.

"Really?" I say. "You've heard about me?"

"Yes," he says, "my big brother won't stop talking about you."

"Wait, what?" I stare in confusion.

"Yes," he adds, "my brother, Simon." His eyes are wide with excitement.

I am floored: this man is just as good looking as Simon, the same features and hair colour, but he seems to have sarcasm in his voice. "Well, I hope it's all good," I say. He smiles and I see a lot of Simon in him it's uncanny; I'm just not sure how they are related. Maybe they share the same father, or perhaps they share their mother's DNA. My head is spinning – how did I not know they were brothers?

"Well," he finally says, "cheers," and he holds up a glass of champagne.

I hold up my empty glass and smile. I say, "Cheers, but sorry, I'm a vodka drinker."

He laughs and says, "Well, good for you. I personally prefer scotch on the rocks."

I smile as the waiter comes to our table and I choose the mustard-stuffed chicken because I know I need to eat something. We all have our empty wine glasses filled and at this point I think I'll drink anything. I need to find Simon: I need him by my side, I need his support. I ask the waitress if I could possibly have a vodka, to which she smiles politely and wanders off in the direction of the bar. Cecile is chatting to a man to her left and Jonathan is talking to some blonde to his right. I sit here feeling like an idiot, and when my vodka arrives I down it and ask for another one. There is music playing in the background: Leona Lewis singing about being happy – but it's low and soft. The lights are dipping from purple to yellow to green and pink, and when the food arrives it smells so good I eat nearly everything on my plate like I've not eaten for a year. Why the fuck can't I see Simon – or Celina for that matter? Mervin and Miles are on the next table from me and look just as glum; they seem to be between two people who look old. I need to leave, I need air, but as I call the waitress over for another drink, the music dips and the lights come up, and up on stage is the ever-beautiful Celina. She is a vision, and I hear Jonathan say, "Fuck me, I'll have a glass of that!" and I cringe.

She taps the mic and says, "Good evening, everyone. Thank you so much for joining us this evening. We have a couple of special guests I would like to introduce; without them none of this would have been possible; without them we wouldn't be in this stunning hall, eating this beautiful food, so please join me in welcoming them onto the stage – Mr Hails and Mr Boon."

Everyone starts to clap and Jonathan gets up from my side and walks towards the stage. I see Simon rise from five tables away and start to walk over to his brother, and I clap along. Cecile is way too enthusiastic to my left, and I fear she may break her hands.

They both climb the stairs to get on stage, playfully fighting each other as they go. Jonathan takes the mic from Celina, kissing her on the cheek, and speaking first, saying, "Welcome, everyone, thank you to the beautiful Celina – she does a fantastic job being Simon's right hand man, so to speak, and I for one think he's a very lucky man to have her at his beck and call." Everyone cheers, and I can't help but sink into my seat slightly and hold my stomach at the thought of them together. "We are happy to have you all here to help join us in celebrating the sexy new line. It's been a few weeks of hard graft and lots of negotiations, which my brother will tell you about. I'm just the other brother who sits and looks pretty."

Everyone laughs as Simon steps forward and pokes his brother in the side. He looks so beautiful up there! Jonathan hands the mic to Simon, who starts to speak passionately. "Yes, the negotiations have been long and hard," he says, and when he says hard he looks directly at me and I blush and sink more into my chair. "We have a fantastic team, and yes, I am a lucky man to have the beautiful Celina, who is ruthless in getting what she wants. She has done a great job with the location and the décor, and all the finer details." Celina blows him a kiss and the room cheers again. "Then there are Miles and Mervin, our web designers. If I didn't know them any better, I'd say they were married! But really, guys, well done on the advert. If at any time you want some privacy, we can all leave!" Everyone in the room laughs and claps. Mervin holds up his hand as if to say 'thank you', while Miles just puts his hand on his head as if to show his embarrassment. "We have the beautiful Cecile, who has been by my side the entire time. She is the one we have to thank for choosing the wonderful food this evening; so thank you, Cecile.

"Of course, most of you know our father passed away recently and my team have stepped up and taken control, so thank you. But, of course, the star of this whole show is none other than the stunning Ruby Frankton, so please put your hands together as we welcome her on stage."

Oh, shit, oh, fuck! Here we go. All eyes are on me as I stand, and my legs feel like mush. Everyone is clapping, but I want to be sick. I smile and move as best I can to the stage: one step at a time, Ruby. I feel so elegant walking past flashing lights towards the stage, but at the same time I feel a fool. Simon greets me as I walk up the steps and tells me to calm down and breathe – my face must say it all. He kisses my cheek again and says, "You've got this." He smells so good, I want to take him here on the stage. Jonathan kisses me, too, and I can smell his clothes and it's the same aftershave I've grown to love.

I take to the mic and freeze. I can't really see anyone because the lights are so bright. "Good evening," I say. "Sorry if I stutter – I'm actually quite crap at public speaking, and I apologise if I faint!" Everyone laughs. "So I'm here because I had, well, an opinion. Some of you may scratch your head at this and wonder how this all came to be from an opinion. Well, you see, being a larger woman, so to speak," I say, putting my hands on my waist. "Some may call me a chunky butt!" Again they laugh. "I found that sexy lingerie should be more adaptable for the larger ladies and advertising should not be aimed at skinny people – sorry to all the skinny people who are here, but looking at you wearing sexy undies will not make me want to get up off the sofa to exercise just so I can wear that skimpy little thong that I'll probably look like a beached whale in." Again more muffled laughs. "I guess what I'm trying to say is, if I want to look and feel sexy, I also need to be comfortable. I want to feel comfortable and look sexy at the same time. I want to know the underwear I'm wearing is going to hide a million sins, not convict me of them; and, well, I think this new line has done that. The colours are fab and the prints even better – so thank you, Runaway Lingerie, for making me feel sexy but in a more dignified manner." I smile. "Thank you to Simon and Jonathan for giving me a chance and believing in my opinions. I've loved every minute," and when I say that, I turn and look at Simon, who's smiling hard. "Thank you again," I say, giving a slight curtsy, as everyone claps and I turn again to lock eyes with Simon. 'Okay, Ruby,' I say in my head, 'you fucking nailed it!'

I step back and Jonathan kisses my cheek a bit too enthusiastically, as Simon watches wide-eyed, and then he kisses me, too, whispering in my ear, "That was some speech."

Celina steps forward and tells everyone, "Please enjoy the rest of your evening; drink and be merry."

We all exit the stage and the music kicks in: Lana del Rey sings 'Born To Die'. I walk to my table and down the drink that is waiting for me. Simon has been pulled towards the door by various people, while Jonathan has got his hand on some blonde at the next table – I'm presuming it's his girlfriend, but then I'm guessing he's not a faithful boyfriend type.

Cecile congratulates me on a good speech, and I tell her I was nearly sick, but I'm glad I held it together. I see Mervin looking at me, waving and saying 'good job'. I put my hand up to wave and then point my finger to the bar, to which he nods, so we walk past Simon, who watches me closely, but I refuse to look at him – this is my time now. I order two shots of Sambuca, and we say cheers as we down it. I'm feeling tipsy, but we order another one for luck, as Mervin congratulates me on an awesome speech. I shake my head and say that it was fucking scary, but then, feeling brave, I head back into the hall and on to the dance floor, just as Jonathan comes up behind me. Solomon Burke sings 'Cry To Me' as Jonathan grabs me around my waist. My arms go around his shoulders, and we grind on each other, and I can see Simon watching my every move. Jonathan sure can dance: he is big and strong and sexy, and my tipsy eyes are sending me crazy. Jonathan spins me around and I laugh, but when I look again, Simon has gone and my heart breaks. The song finishes and I thank him for the dance, then I walk away. The blonde from our table comes along and takes my place.

I have to find Simon and tell him I still need him, but first I need another drink. I grab my bag from under my seat and head for the bar. I see Mervin is still there as I head back. "Tequila?" he shouts. I give a thumbs-up, and when it arrives I neck it. It's disgusting, I hate the stuff.

"Have you seen Simon?" I ask.

He looks puzzled and says, "I think he went that way," pointing to the lobby.

"Okay, thanks for the drink," I shout, walking in the direction of the lobby. I pass people who are talking about the show, and how well Simon and

Jonathan have done for themselves. It's cooler near the door, and there is a face on reception I don't know: where is the smiling Thomas, I wonder? I can hear voices down the hall, so I head that way, and as I turn the corner I see Celina step forward and kiss Simon, and it's like time has stood still. I freeze. Fuck, shit! Simon pushes Celina back, shocked.

"Oh, god, I'm so sorry," I say.

Simon looks at me and, closing his eyes, he mouths the word 'fuck'. I quickly turn to leave and Simon pushes past Celina, calling my name. "Ruby, wait!" he yells. Celina looks shocked.

I reach the elevator and press the button. Please, please hurry, I say. I'm begging the elevator to get to me before he does. It pings and the doors slide open. I climb in and turn around just as the doors shut, but an arm comes through the gap – it's Simon. He pulls the doors open and steps inside, looking straight at me. The doors shut behind him, as he starts to speak. "Ruby, please, it's not what you think."

I hold up my hand. "Please, it's none of my fucking business."

"Ruby, don't do that," he begs. "*Please*. Celina kissed me; I didn't kiss her back," he adds.

"I don't care," I say with conviction. "Simon, I don't fucking care," and with that, he smacks the emergency button so the elevator can't go anywhere.

"Ruby, I'm telling you the truth," he yells.

"Okay, Simon, I believe you," I say. "That's

great," I add.

He looks at me straight-faced. "Ruby what do you want from me?" he asks.

"What do I want, Simon? I'm angry. What do you fucking think I want?" I stare wildly. "I know, how about this?" I scream. "What do you fucking want, Simon? Cos I don't think it's me. Tell me what you fucking want," I add.

He clenches his fists and runs his hands through his hair. "Ruby, what do you want me to say?" He's mad and frustrated. "You want me to say I fucking love you." He's so fucking hot and conflicted. "You want me to say how much I've fallen in fucking love with you and that I can't see myself ever being without you. Is that what you want me to say? Okay, fine," he says, throwing his hands up in the air, "I fucking love you. I love you so much it fucking hurts. I love you so much I can't stop thinking about you. I want to kiss you and touch you all the fucking time, but I can't, I just fucking can't," and with that he falls back against the wall.

I'm stunned and I can't move. "Simon," I finally say, "if I knew it would cause you so much heartache, I would have walked away. I just need you to explain to me why. Why can't you? What's stopping you? I need to know; help me understand." I want to cry: I want to cry for me, and cry for him; this is all too much.

He steps closer and grabs me around my waist,

kissing me long and hard. I sense the need to feel me close; I need to feel him, too. He pushes me back against the elevator wall, and we are breathing heavy, with a new sense of love and want. I drop my bag and I grab his hair and he pushes his hard groin against me. "I need to fuck you, Ruby," he says with heated breath. I love this man and would let him do anything at this precise moment. He growls in my ear, "Ruby, let me fuck you, please," and he tells me it won't take long, and this makes me smile.

He puts his right hand between my legs and grabs my wet throbbing pussy, his fingers poking through my lace thong and making circles on my clit, over and over, then pressing his palm against me, rubbing hard. I spread my legs to give him more access. My new knickers are soaked, but I'm so fucking horny as he pulls them to the side and puts his middle finger deep inside me, and back on my clit, again and again, kissing me hard. I come hard violently. "I fucking need you," he murmurs.

I kiss him harder and say, "Well then, take me." He grabs my new thong with both hands and rips it off, undoes his flies and pulls out his hard cock. He looks deep in my eyes and I know he is all I'll ever want; then he lifts the front ruffles of my dress and rams his cock deep inside me. I feel all of him, as he holds me up by cupping my bare buttocks and he rotates his hips, around and around; he is relentless, and he loves me. I grip his shoulders, pulling him close so he can fuck me harder than ever. With a new need, he hardens and comes aggressively, growling my name, breathing heavily, slowing to a stop, his breathing coming to a calm rhythm.

"I am yours, Mr Hails!"

He squeezes my butt cheeks and sighs. "No, Ruby Frankton, it is I that am yours."

We pull apart and I'm so wet between my legs, but he pulls a napkin from his pocket and hands it to me. "Sorry," he says with a sheepish look. I smile and put it between my legs. My thong lies on the floor, ruined, so he picks it up and puts it in his pocket and says sorry again, then steps back against the wall. I can see he's in pain as he tucks himself in and straightens his bow-tie.

"What are you not telling me, Simon?" I ask. He looks lost. "Talk to me," I say, stepping forward. He sighs and looks me deep in my eyes, his face full of pain, and after an age he tells me we can't be together. "Wait, what? Simon, I don't understand."

He sighs again. "Look, my father was a very complicated man – some may say a selfish man – but his dying wish was for me to marry and have children." He looks so sad when he speaks.

"Okay," I say, all confused, "that's not so bad."

"No, Ruby, you don't understand. He became a very wealthy man at a young age; he made his money selling some of the finest jewellery to the rich and famous."

"Okay, but why did that make him selfish?" I say,
all confused.

"Okay, when I was a baby, my father cheated on
my mother and when she found out about Jonathan
she banned my father from having any access, and
they paid Jonathan's mother a lump sum to stay away.
My father had no choice but to agree, because a lot of
the businesses are in joint ownership and if my
mother had wanted to, she could have taken my father
for every penny. Over the years she became more
bitter and twisted, so she made my father draw up his
will stating his son, that's me" – he points to himself
– "will inherit the business and all his fortune after his
death; but – and there's a but, Ruby – I was not to
marry or be with anyone who already has children by
another man. I am to find a girl not tainted by
marriage or having carried a child in her womb, and
then when my first-born child is brought into this
world, and only then, will I be able to claim my
inheritance; and if I fall in love with someone who has
children by another man, I will be cast out of the
family and I will have nothing."

"Oh," I say. I'm stunned and I'm angry and I'm
sad for him all at the same time.

"I would walk away from it all, Ruby, I would;
but my father's dying wish to me was to make sure
Jonathan and I are set for life. He never wanted to
leave Jonathan without a father, but my mother
insisted; so when he asked me to go find Jonathan a

few years ago, we became inseparable. My father loaned us the money to start our business, because he wanted us to do well and become partners – so that's what we did; and although Jonathan never met our father, he never held a grudge. He has never felt hate, just love. My mother placed my father in a care home a few months back when his Alzheimer's became too much; then we were given the news he only had a few weeks to live due to cancer. I've been by his side, Ruby, I've been with him every evening, every weekend, caring for him, reading to him, telling him all about you, telling him how in love I am, and how I want to be with you and marry you."

"Wow," I say, all shocked. "Marry? Wait, what?"

"I could see how much this pained my father, but he made me promise, and I'm so sorry, Ruby, truly I am. That's why I haven't stayed with you; that's why I always leave you; and that's why I won't get too close; but believe me, I want to, I just can't." He shakes his head, so I move closer to him and he pulls me into his embrace, and for a brief moment I think I heard him cry. My own tears are finally flowing. "Do you know the sad part?" he sighs, and I look up at him. "I still love my mother; I still want to take care of her and tell her I love her; and to this day she does not know Jonathan is my brother – she thinks he's just a business partner; but if she were to find out about you, we would lose the business. She would take it all away."

I reach my hands up and touch his soft face. "Of course you love her, Simon, she's your mother. She didn't plan for your father to cheat, she didn't plan for another child to be born; she's angry and bitter and I guess you could say I don't blame her. But you know you could walk away." I smile at him. "You could walk away from it all and we could make our own fortune." I kiss him and tell him that as long as we have each other, we can make it.

He looks in my eyes and wipes away a tear with his thumb, and I see the look of sadness on his face. "Yes, we could do that, we could walk away; but then I have gone against my father's dying wish," he finally says, "and my brother gets nothing, and he deserves better. I'm sorry, truly I am, but I just can't; and as much as it pains me to walk away, it's what I have to do."

"Wait, what? What do you mean, Simon? What do you mean, walk away?" I step back. "You're scaring me now," I say. As he stands, he pulls a cheque from inside his jacket pocket and hands it to me. I open it and look in amazement: the cheque is for fifty thousand pounds! "What's this for?" I say.

He smiles weakly and says, "It's your bonus, a share of the profits. Ruby, I asked you to help with this new line because I knew at some point I would have to walk." As he holds his hands up, he says, "I never thought this day would actually come, but it's because of my feelings for you I have to leave. I need to know you're going to be okay."

I look back at the cheque. "Simon, I don't want your money – I want you. Please don't do this."

He comes close to me once more and kisses me softly on the lips. "I'm so sorry," he whispers. He stands back near the wall and unclips the emergency stop, all the time looking at me. "I need to rejoin the party, I need to find Celina and explain it's not going to happen."

I look at him, stunned. "You're leaving me again!" I drop my arms and close my eyes as the doors open.

He turns and says, "Hey, we are friends, yeah?" He turns and leaves, and I'm rooted; I can't do anything.

I mumble, "Yeah, and you're still my boss." I can't make my feet walk, so when the doors close once more, I press the button for floor three. I'm numb. I've detached myself once again.

CHAPTER EIGHTEEN

Picking up my bag as the elevator announces the third floor, I stumble to my door and pull out my keycard from my purse. I swipe it and go inside, and as the door slams behind me, I sink to the floor. I have lost him, I have lost everything, and now he's gone. My heart hurts, like I've been punched in the chest. I crawl out of my dress and over to my suitcase, then slip on some sweats, chucking the wet hanky from between my legs in the corner, and I put on a t-shirt. I find my phone and try to call him, but his number goes to voicemail. I try to message him, telling him to please don't do this, but it goes unanswered. I can't breathe – I need my girls, I need a drink, I need to sleep. Fuck, what do I need? I need him.

I crawl up on the bed and cry. I sob so loudly I think they could hear me downstairs, but eventually I fall asleep, waking with a start and grabbing my phone. It's 3am. I sit up, feeling light-headed. I don't hear anything: I don't hear music, just silence. I decide to go down to the lobby to see if there is anyone around. I need to see if Simon is still here.

The elevator takes me down, and I don't care about what I've got on. The doors open and I step into a dimmed lobby. A young woman at reception looks up at me and asks if I need help with anything. I shake my head and walk towards the bar. Everywhere is quiet, with just a few drunks sitting at a table, mumbling to each other about the world. I walk up to the bar and I'm surprised when I see Michelle. She comes over and says hello.

"Please may I have a double vodka with a dash of Coke?" I say.

She smiles and says, "I'm sorry, I'm not allowed to serve any more alcohol tonight."

I smile and say, "Look, I've had a pretty crap night. I just want one drink and then I'll leave, I promise."

With that, she takes a deep breath and smiles, saying, "Okay, just one."

I smile back and wait for my drink. She hands it to me and smiles. Taking my glass in hand, I wander into the hall; it's empty and the lights are off. I walk slowly around all the tables, thinking how pretty they had looked earlier – now they lay wrecked, with empty glasses and dirty napkins – and when I get to Simon's table, I stop when I see his name tag. I pick it up and put it in my pocket – I don't know why; it just feels nice to have his name close to me. Silly, really.

I then walk to my table and pick up my name tag and put that in my pocket, too. I finish my drink in the quiet, dark room, then head back to the lobby to call the elevator. Maybe all will be clear tomorrow; maybe I will wake up from this crap dream and Simon will still want me.

Back in my room, I pick up my beautiful dress and pop it back in its bag. I hang it in the closet and I pick up the cheque off the floor and sit on the bed. I look at the figure and sigh. "What the hell do I want with all this money?" I say out loud. How will work be on Monday; how will I tell my girls; what about Celina? Oh god, my head is fogging again. I climb into bed without even brushing my teeth, and I soon sink into a deep, troubled sleep. I'm falling, and Celina is laughing at me. Simon stands with his hands in his pockets, watching me, and I'm dancing with Jonathan around and around till I'm so dizzy I wake up soaked in sweat. I sit up feeling sick, and run to the bathroom and throw up in the toilet. Not a lot comes up, because I've not eaten since the night before.

Walking back into the room, I fill the kettle and make myself a tea. Suddenly, there's a knock on my door and it makes me jump and my stomach twist. What if it's Simon? What if he's come back? I walk to the door and look through the peep hole: it's Celina. Shit, fuck, bollocks! She knocks again, so I decide to open the door, and when she sees my face she smiles shyly. "Good morning, Ruby," she says. I put up a hand as if to say hi. "Look, I wanted to explain about last night…"

I hold up my hand again and say, "Please stop,

Celina, you don't have to explain anything."

"No, please," she adds, "I do. I'm so sorry I didn't tell you what was about to happen with Simon. I have had these crazy feelings for him for so long, I couldn't stop myself. I just needed him to know and, well, when I kissed him last night and you just happened to come round the corner at that very same moment…" I close my eyes at the thought, as she stops and sighs. "Well, the look on Simon's face when you saw us was like a bolt of lightning really; and, well, when he explained his feelings for you, I wasn't at all surprised. I mean, you're smart and funny and, well, just a bloody nice person."

"Wait, what? Simon told you about us?"

"Well, no" – she gives me an awkward smile – "not exactly. He just said he has a strong pull towards you, but with his mother's wishes he was finding things difficult; and I'm sorry, Ruby, but I don't really know what he meant, so I just said sorry and he walked away. It was all rather strange" I tell her I'm not feeling well and I need to shower, to which she apologises again and says, "Well, don't let me keep you. Some of us are having breakfast before we leave, if you would care to join us." I say no, thank you, to which she says, "Okay. Well, we will see you at work on Monday then.

I smile and say, "Yes, you sure will." She gives a little wave and I shut the door. Stripping naked, I shower until the water wrinkles my fingers. I just don't want to do anything – I want him, and he is all I'll ever want. I turn off the shower, dry and dress. 'What the hell, Ruby?' I scold myself. 'Why didn't you go after him last night; why didn't you fight?' But my inner bitch has gone away: there is no fight left. I can't make him stay.

I remove the napkin from the other side of the room and put it in the bin, then pack my case and grab my dress from the closet. Walking to the elevator with a heavy heart, I push the button for the ground floor, and I can't help but look around me: how can such a small space hold such trauma?

I walk past reception, laying down my keycard as I go, not even bothering to see who's on the desk or say 'thank you'. I walk straight and I walk briskly out of the building to my car, sling everything in the boot and climb in, pulling my seatbelt on and starting the car. The radio springs into life, playing Phil Collins's 'I Wish It Would Rain Down'.

I exit the car park and hit the open road, and I cry the whole way down the dual carriageway heading home. I can't wait to see my girls; I've missed them so much. I've decided to tell them everything, and I'm absolutely bricking it, because they will hate Simon and I don't want that.

Pulling into my street, I park my car, empty the boot and head inside. My house feels good; it smells like home, and this is where I'm safe. I drop my stuff by the door and go to the kitchen and grab a drink.

Yes, it's early, but I don't care; the way I see it, if I was on holiday and it was two o'clock, I would be drinking by the pool. Maybe that's what I need – a holiday. Maybe I should use the money Simon gave me and leave town, move abroad and start again. But what about the girls? I will miss them too much.

I collapse on the sofa and stay there all afternoon. I can't get Simon off my mind. Right from the start, he has played with my emotions; then right at the end he tells me he loves me. What a crock of shit that was! We can't be together and that's heart-breaking.

My phone rings, waking me from my daydream, and it's Jessica. "Hey, mum," she screams, "we are coming over now, if you're home."

"Yes!" I cry. "Yes, I'm home, come now! I miss you guys so much."

"Okay, see you in a bit."

"Okay, sweetheart, love you."

"Love you, mum," shouts Belle in the background.

I hang up the phone and go grab my case and dress that are still near the front door, and I take them upstairs and throw my dress in the closet, giving it a kick for good measure. Okay, okay, I'm angry, I know. I don't mean it; it's a beautiful dress.

Thirty minutes later, the door bursts open and in come my babies. "Mum!" they say, as I come from the kitchen. We throw ourselves at each other and I just can't help bursting into tears. "Oh, mum," they say, "what's wrong? We have only been gone two weeks."

I say, "I know," through outbursts of sobbing. "I have so much to tell you guys."

"Oh, mum," they say.

It's been ages since I've even spoke with anyone about love and feeling and meeting a man, so I don't know where to start. My girls sit and listen and nod and cry and laugh and then get angry and then hug me. It's a rollercoaster! I tell them how in love I am and they smile.

Belle says, "Mum, if he can't leave his family for you, then he's a prick."

I laugh and say, "See, this is why I don't tell you anything! He really isn't a prick, Belle – he is a headfuck, but he's not a prick," I say through tears. "He wants to follow his father's dying wish," I add.

Then Jessica slaps Belle on the arm and says, "Yeah, Belle, stop being so inconsiderate."

We laugh again and finally get up off the floor. "I think my butt has fallen asleep," I say. "Okay, so how was your holiday?"

"Please, mum, we don't care about that now; we want to talk about you and Mr I-can't-commit," says Belle with a screwed-up face.

I chuck a cushion at her and say, "Stop!"

She laughs and says, "Sorry, I can't help it if I think he's an idiot, mum."

"We had a fantastic time," Jessica smiles. "The

weather was lush and so were the men!" Jessica laughs hard, and when I say "Men?", she adds, "I mean the one Belle had in her bed nearly every night!"

Belle chucks the cushion back at Jessica. "Stop! Mum doesn't need to hear that!"

I give a big sigh and tell them, "But I actually do, just as long as you were careful. I'm not ready to be a granny just yet!" and we all laugh again.

Come six o'clock, the girls announce that they must get home to sort their laundry and get ready for work tomorrow, but not before pulling out of Belle's bag a beautiful ceramic bowl painted in stunning Greek hieroglyphics. "Oh, I love it!" I say. "Thank you. I love you, guys," I say, hugging them.

"And we love you. Remember, if you need us, just call, okay?"

I see them out of the door and wave them down the street, before walking back in and shutting the door, when the reality of being alone comes flooding back and I start crying again. I need a drink, so the rest of the night consists of vodka, love songs and crisps. I join in loudly with The Verve's 'The Drugs Don't Work'. In my drunken state, holding up my vodka, I screech, "Yes, it does work – it makes me forget, and I need to forget."

CHAPTER NINETEEN

Finally, midnight comes and I collapse in bed. I don't even undress, and I've still got my boots on, when the alarm rings, telling me it's Monday morning, and I need to get up and go to work. My head hurts, but it's all just a reminder of how I feel lost and just want him back.

I slowly shower and dress in my black skirt and my soft pink sweater. I don't know why I pick that; maybe because there's a tiny glimmer of hope that he will be at the office, and I want him to see me looking hot and for him to see what he's missing. I climb in my for-now car, telling myself I need to buy a new car so this one can go back; but deep down I love this one and it will be hard to give it back.

Parking in the car park, I don't see his car, and that makes my heart sink. I just wish I could see him, or hear his voice, or feel his touch once more. I hold my head high and walk in.

Cecile smiles and says, "Good morning, Ruby."

I smile back and say, "Good morning."

The boys both wave and say 'hi', but soon look back at their screens. Celina comes from Simon's office and says, "Good morning, Ruby, you look lovely today."

I say, "Thank you and good morning."

"So, at 9.30 I would like everyone in the office for a briefing, okay?" She puts up a thumb as if to soften the blow of what's about to be said.

Yes, I nod, walking over to the coffee machine, my head still banging from last night. I make my tea and sit at my desk, and don't do anything for thirty minutes – I just sit there, staring at nothing. I can't be here: the memories are just too much.

Celina breaks my thoughts. "Ready?" she smiles.

I say, "Yes," and stand, walking into the other room. We all take a seat at the big table and wait for Celina to speak.

"Okay, so first of all, thank you so much for Saturday. We have had an amazing response to the new line; the feedback was phenomenal. We have hit over half a million pounds in online orders alone, and that's just one weekend. It's crazy!" she laughs.

"Wow, that is absolutely crazy," I smile. "We actually did it!"

"Ruby, your speech was fantastic, and it clearly got people talking. They loved seeing the passion of your vision; so thank you from all of us. But, guys," she adds, "everyone has pulled together and we couldn't have done it without each and every one of your skills and input, so thank you. The second thing I need to discuss is a bit more depressing. Unfortunately, Simon won't be coming back to work for a while…"

'Wait, what?' my head is screaming.

"He's taking some personal time off to look after his mother." She looks directly at me and continues, "He's had some personal issues lately and he wants to have some time away to get his life in check, and I've been asked to stand in for him and I've been promoted to managing director."

Cecile and the boys start clapping and I follow.

"Well done," says Cecile, "that's fantastic news." Then she looks at me.

"Yeah, well done you," says Mervin. "Now I can tell people I've actually got a hot boss!" He and Miles high-five each other.

I'm speechless. Taking time off from what? Me? For how long? Will he come back? Will he just leave and I'll never see him again?

Celina looks at me while everyone is chatting and mouths 'Are you okay?' I slowly nod and rise from my chair, heading to the kitchen; I need to get away from this room, I need to leave this building. I can't do this without him; I need him here where I can see him and touch him.

Cecile follows me to the kitchen and puts her hand on my shoulder. "I'm so sorry, Ruby," she says. "I know you two had something special. I could see it in his eyes and the way you both look at each other."

I feel like crying. "What am I going to do now?" I say. "Where has he gone?"

"I don't know," Cecile replies. "I've never seen him like this." She shakes her head and keeps rubbing my shoulder, but it's not helping. It's just not fair.

By three o'clock, I'm done. I can't stand this, so I decide to tell Celina I'm going home.

She nods and says, "It's understandable. Take as much time as you need."

I drive into town and deposit my cheque in the bank, the cashier looking at me in amazement, and I can't help but think, 'Yeah, it's only money, love.'

Back home, I call the girls. I tell them I've decided to move, and they are both in shock, but understand why. I tell them I need somewhere far away from the memories.

"Okay," says Belle, "where are you going?"

"I don't know yet, but I know I need to leave Norwich," I say. "I'm thinking about going to live by the sea."

"Wow!" says Jessica. "Are you sure, mum?"

"Yes, I've never been so sure," I reply. "Besides, living on the coast means some beautiful scenery, and maybe having the beach on my doorstep might make me do some more exercise," I laugh. "I just need to do it. I need to sort my life out. I can't keep moping around thinking of him."

"Well, we will be with you the whole time," says Jessica, "and I think it's great what you're doing," she adds.

So that night I don't have a lot to drink for the

first time in, like, forever. I need to be sober if I'm going to make big decisions.

The next morning, I phone work and tell them I'm not coming back. Celina puts me on speaker-phone; she is very understanding and tells me I will be missed.

And Cecile is not surprised when she comes on the phone. "I knew you would walk. I knew it after the show at the hotel. I wish you all the luck in the world. Stay in touch, and I hope you get your happy ending," she adds.

The boys shout out, "Nice knowing you, piss head!"

And I shout back, "That's what your dad said when I left his bed this morning!"

They all laugh, and Mervin shouts, "Who's dad, though?"

I say, "Thanks for making me feel welcome, guys," and they all say goodbye. I hang up the phone and take a deep breath. Next, I phone the estate agent: a woman answers and she's super-helpful and tells me she can come out tomorrow for an assessment. I tell her I want a quick sale, no messing, as I need to be gone.

She says, "Okay, would today be too soon?"

I say, "No, today would be perfect"; so come one o'clock, she's in my living room, looking around and measuring walls and checking for damp and cracks. She walks upstairs and into the three spacious bedrooms and a fully functioning bathroom, minus one lock on the bathroom door, and she writes stuff on her notepad and smiles at me a lot. She asks me why the quick sale, and I tell her I have family by the sea. It's a lie, of course, but then I tell her I need to move closer to them, and her face lights up.

"Well, as it happens," she says, "my nephew lives in Boston, and, well, he sells property. He's very good and he will get you a perfect little cottage by the sea if you're wanting a better life, so to speak."

I clap my hands and say 'perfect', so she hands me a number and tells me, "We won't have trouble selling your house; it's very well looked after, it's spacious and well decorated." With that, she leaves and I smile at the thought of a fresh start.

I spend the next few weeks in limbo. I stop drinking and even start exercising – crazy how a man or the lack of one can make you do crazy things. I've already lost weight from not eating, and I've not thought of Simon at all. That's a lie – he's on my mind all the time. I think of his kiss, his touch, his beautiful body close to mine; I cry all the time – like I mean all the time – I miss him so much it kills me. I think about messaging him all the time, but then I delete it.

After four weeks on the market, my house sells for way more than I hoped and I'm so happy and excited, I call the girls and they scream down the phone with happiness. Now all I have to do is find a house by the sea.

"Mum, we wish you all the luck in the world and we will be cheering you on from Norfolk – and, well, the weekend trips will be fantastic! We can help you get sorted with everything: we will help pack the moving truck, we will be with you every step of the way and give you a big send-off."

I tell them it's going to be tough leaving them, to which they say they are big enough and ugly enough to look after themselves. I phone the estate agent in Boston and spend the next hour deciding where I'd like to go. We settle on Butterwick, because that's what I have in my head and I like the name. With only a short drive to the long white sandy beaches, it's a quiet little village and, well, I can just blend in, start again, and maybe even get a little dog to keep me company. I'm so excited; the girls will be able to come visit frequently, as it is near but far enough away. I agree to go up there for a visit at the weekend to look around some properties; the girls would love to come, but they have to work.

I book myself into the local Butterwick Bush hotel; and they even have a pool. If I don't do it now, I never will, and I'll always be stuck here wanting Simon. So Friday night comes and I'm driving up the A17, heading over the Sutton bridge. I'm super-excited for the weekend of house-hunting, and it's the first time I've been anywhere since the hotel show, and the first time I've thought of Simon in days. Just when I think I'm over it, I get another wallop in the face. I've never felt this way about anyone in my life, and again it hurts my heart.

CHAPTER TWENTY

I arrive at the hotel just after six o'clock and I'm greeted at reception with a warm smile and a hello.

"Wow, your hotel is lovely," I say, "really warm and homely." A three-seater couch is in front of an open fire, and I bet in the winter it looks amazing. There is a grandfather clock at the bottom of the stairs to the right of the reception desk and a bar to the left, down a small passageway.

"Well, thank you. Please call me Kate," says the older-looking lady. She has short white hair and she reminds me of Dame Judi Dench. "I'm guessing you're Miss Frankton?" she asks, and I say 'yes'. "Well, welcome," she smiles. "I hope your journey wasn't a bad one. Now, would you like a robe for your room?"

I smile and say, "Yes, please."

"What size would you like?" she asks. "We have small, medium, lovely or extra lovely."

I can't help but giggle and say, "Extra lovely, please."

She grabs one from the large closet next to the clock and hands it to me. "If you need anything, don't hesitate to call down, okay?" she adds.

I smile and say, "Thank you. Are there certain times I can use the pool?" I ask.

"Oh, no, feel free to dip whenever; it's heated, so you won't freeze." She smiles, hands me a key and tells me, "You're up the stairs to the right, and breakfast will be served between seven and ten."

I smile and grab my bag from the floor. Taking my key, I head up the stairs to room 11. It's quite spacious and warm, and smells of fresh linen. A king-size bed dominates the room, with white covers and a soft blue throw over one corner – it does look inviting – and I have my own bathroom, which is nice. I look out of my window and see the pool: it looks so pretty all lit up in the dark.

I unpack my case and head down for a swim. Everywhere is quiet, although I can hear a few people chatting in the bar; but I bypass all of that and head outside into the cool night air. There is a small changing block near one end of the pool which has a bench inside to lay your things on, and a curtain to pull across for your dignity. I change and walk to the pool. Since losing weight, I've treated myself to a bikini: it's white and the bottoms have laces on either side to tie them up; the top is frilly and makes my breasts look good.

I dive into the pool and it's a perfect temperature. I swim a few lengths and then rest my arms on the edge, looking up at the night sky. It's so peaceful here; I could get used to this. I decide on a few more lengths, then I'll head in for some food. But as I come back from the second lap, I'm aware there is someone standing at the end of the pool with his hands in his pockets and, oh my, that breathtaking smile I know so well! It's Simon, and I almost choke on the water and nearly drown. Holy fuck! No, it can't be. I'm in shock and I just float in the pool, trying not to go under.

"Hello, Ruby," he says.

I don't speak. He smiles and lowers himself to a squat, resting his arms on his strong legs, his head tilted to one side. I just stare at him. "Well, say something," he says; but I can't. I can't move; I need to leave; no, I need him to leave. We just stare at each other for a long time, then I swim to the edge of the pool and climb up the metal steps. I know he's watching me with heated eyes as I walk past him to the changing block and grab my towel, and when I spin around he's right in front of me.

"Ruby, please say something"; but I don't. I wrap my towel around me and go to pick up my bag, but he grabs my arm. "Goddammit, Ruby, talk to me!"

I yank his arm away and look deep into his eyes. I shake my head and say, "I can't. You need to leave, please," and in a small voice I add, "I can't do this again," and I close my eyes.

He steps forward, pushing me back into the changing block, and pulls the curtain shut. He undoes my towel and it drops to the floor, as he runs his hands down my arms and holds my hands. I stand looking at his chest. I think my heart is going to beat out of my body. "Look at me, Ruby," he says in a calm, sexy voice, and as I look up to the man I love, he kisses me – he kisses me so gently and slowly. I squeeze his hands, and he feels so good; and that smell I know so well fills my nose, awakening my senses. He releases his grip and then pulls on the string either side of my bikini bottoms. They slide away from me onto the floor, revealing my now naked bottom. He unclips my top and lets it fall away, then reaches round and cups my buttocks, squeezing hard. I move my hands up to his waist and undo the buttons on his trousers. I can feel his cock already hard and in desperate need to be freed. He reaches around and grabs my breasts; he stops kissing me and puts my left breast in his mouth, gently sucking on my nipple. I release him from his trousers and stroke his smooth, hard erection. He kisses me again and turns himself so he is sitting on the bench, then pulls me towards him so I'm sitting astride his lap. I gently lower myself onto his pulsating manhood. I wrap my arms around him and hold on, as he kisses me, invading my mouth with his tongue. I rotate my hips around and around. He is so fucking hot! I love this man with my very soul. I moan into his mouth as I feel my orgasm rise, and we are lost in one another as he grabs my buttocks and moves me faster. He, too, is moaning between kisses, as we lock eyes and I stop kissing him, placing my forehead on his – but I don't stop moving. He moans through gritted teeth as I pull his hair with both hands.

"You feel so good," he growls. "I need to have you all the time. I need you to come for me, come for me, Ruby, please!" And with that, he kisses me again and I come long and hard, convulsing like a giant earthquake, and in that very moment he comes, too, grabbing my waist and pulling me close, saying, Fuck, fuck, fuck!"

I feel the room spinning. I've never felt so good – he makes me come alive, he makes everything better. When our breathing slows and we come down from our orgasms, I look at him. "Simon, why are you here? How did you know I was here?" I say, out of breath. "How did you know to find me?"

He smiles and says, "I've had the pleasure of meeting your beautiful girls…"

Wait, what? I shoot back away from him. "How?" I say, all shocked.

He smiles again and tells me, "I went to your house and started banging on your door, then I tried calling you, but it wouldn't connect."

I look down and say, "Sorry, I blocked your number."

He smiles and says, "Well, I guessed that. So I'm thinking the neighbour phoned them, because they came over and asked me who I was; and when I told them, they kind of yelled at me a little bit."

"Really?" I say, looking shocked. "I wonder why they would do that?" I add.

He smiles. "They told me where you were, but also said if I hurt you again they will kill me." He looks amused by this, then grabs my arse and tells me I've lost weight.

This makes me beam, but I also tell him, "That's what happens when you have your heart broken." He looks sad and tells me he is sorry. "Simon, I'm just in shock, I can hardly speak. What made you come back? I need to know why?"

He shakes his head and kisses me. "Too many questions, Ms Frankton."

"Simon, I need to stand – my knees hurt from the bench," and I can feel myself making a mess all in Simon's groin. I stand and grab my towel, but he gently takes it and uses it to wipe the mess. I smile and shake my head.

"Let's go inside," he says. "Tonight I just want to be close to you," he adds. He grabs my bag and bikini, then we walk inside and up the stairs to my room. I open the door and turn on the lights; it's a dimly lit room, which kind of sets the mood. I throw my towel on the chair and tell him I need to shower, to which he smiles and starts undoing his shirt. I look at him, standing before me, and I can't help but tell him I love him.

He walks over to me and wraps his arms around me, feeling my bare skin. His hands are soft, and he smells heavenly. "Ruby Frankton," he sighs, "I love you with every inch of my body. I don't ever want to be apart from you, and I'm so sorry for breaking your heart."

I put my hands on his face and kiss him. "Please tell me why you're here, Simon. I need to know what's changed. I love that you're here, really I do, but if you suddenly leave again, I don't think I could take it, not again."

"Okay, I will explain, I promise, but let's shower. I will explain it all after that," he adds.

I smile and nod, because I'm just so happy he's here and I'm still in shock. We enter the bathroom and he can't keep his hands to himself, like a naughty teenager. He removes his shirt and trousers and cuddles me from behind, kissing my neck and biting my shoulder. I turn on the shower and he starts running his hands over my shoulders and down to my breasts. His smell is so sweet as he plays with my nipples, twisting and pulling them gently, and I reach around behind me and take his very hard wood in my hands. He moves his hands down to my groin and rubs between my legs. I call out in delight – his touch takes me to places I've never been. We move into the shower and under the water, me facing the wall. I spread my hands on the cold tiles as he plays with my hard clit, dipping his finger in and out of my wet pussy, over and over again. He's kissing my neck and my head is spinning out of control. I tell him I'm going to come, to which he begs me to, spinning me around and pushing his finger in deeper so his palm rotates on my clit. He kisses me all tongues and I come loudly into his mouth. He spins me around again, my orgasm still raging through my body, and he takes me from behind, ploughing into me as I cry out, lifting my right leg so he can go deeper, faster and faster, harder and harder, until he explodes inside me.

He playfully growls in my ear and we are out of breath, we are done. I feel exhausted. I turn to face him and we stand for a few minutes, letting the water wash away our sins. He holds me tight and whispers in my ear that he loves me, and this makes my heart do a double flip. I'm so happy he is here. I tell him I love him, too; then we finish in the shower and head back into the bedroom with towels wrapped around us.

"Simon, please," I say, "I need to know why you're here."

He looks lost as he runs his hand through his hair. "Ruby, I told you I love you and I need to be with you. I was wrong to leave and I should never have walked away – it was one of the worst decisions I've ever made. Look," he says, "I have something for you."

I stand in the middle of the room, looking like I've been struck by lightning. He retrieves something from his jacket, walks back over and stands in front of me and holds out a small box. I look at him in shock. "Simon, what is this?"

He smiles. "Open it, please." He is smiling super hard as I take the box and my hands are shaking. I look at him and then back at the box. I open it slowly and inside is a small gold bracelet, with a flat gold love heart in the centre. It's delicate and beautiful, and I look up at him again and smile. "Read it," he says, "read the heart."

I smile and read: 'we are just friends'. "Oh, Simon," I say, "you've had it engraved in the tiny heart." I smile again.

"Turn it over," he says. He's like a child at Christmas!

I flip it over and engraved on the other side is: 'yes, and I'm your boss'.

"Oh, Simon," I say, "I love it! Thank you." I reach up and wrap my arms around him, hugging him close. He pulls me in tighter than ever, then takes the tiny bracelet from the box and places it around my wrist. He then takes my hand to his mouth and kisses it.

"You hungry?" he asks.

I say, "No, I'm just super-tired."

He nods and says, "Well, in that case, let's go to bed."

"Wait, what? You're staying?" I screech.

He looks at me, puzzled. "Yes. I told you I'm not going anywhere."

I jump in the air and he catches me and my legs wrap around his waist. I feel all giddy, like a teenager who's just got her first boyfriend. He carries me to bed and he lays me down gently so he is on top of me.

"Ruby, if we are to go to bed, you need to let me go."

I shake my head and say, "I will never let you go, Simon Hails!"

He kisses me passionately and I melt into him. We finally climb into bed and I lay in his strong arms and feel his soft chest beneath my cheek. He is breathing gently.

"Simon?" I ask.

"Yes, Ruby," he replies.

"Please tell me what made you decide to come back."

He gives a deep sigh, and rolls onto his side, resting his head on his hand, and I lay next to him with my head on the pillow, waiting for his story. "When I left the hotel that night, I was a mess." He looks hard at me. "I never thought I could feel that way about anyone," he adds. "I spent some time with Jonathan, and he could see the pain in my eyes. Ruby, leaving you nearly killed me." He lies back and runs his hand through his hair as I stroke his chest, trying to comfort him. I lift myself up on my elbow so I can listen intently. "Jonathan told me if I loved you that much, I should just tell my mother the truth, and if it meant being cast out, then so be it. He said he didn't care about the money and that he didn't need it; and he's right, Ruby, we don't need it. But it was my father's wish that was killing me more. I made him a promise. In the end, I decided to go see my mother and tell her about you. I told her I loved you and wanted to be with you. She was angry and hurt and shocked and in total pain – Ruby, the look on her face was unbearable. I thought she was going to kick me out there and then, but she surprised me by saying I should come back to you and try to make things right." I smile and I honestly believe my heart is going to melt. "Ruby," he says, turning over to face me, "I was an idiot; this whole time I've been an idiot. Will you ever forgive me?" I reach up and touch his face and he leans forward and we kiss. "I will never stop wanting you," he adds.

I lay down and snuggle back onto his chest and he holds me tight. I soon fall asleep and sleep peacefully for the first time in months.

CHAPTER TWENTY-ONE

When I wake, I can see the sun is shining through the blinds, but Simon is not lying next to me and I sit up instantly, thinking he's left me again; but when I hear the toilet flush and the door open, my heart stops racing. I touch my chest to calm my breathing as he comes in the room fully dressed and looking damn hot!

"Good morning, Ruby," he says, all cheery.

"Good morning, Simon," I say, stretching.

He sits on the bed next to me and touches my cheek. He smells delicious. "I have to go, I'm afraid."

I make a sad face and ask if everything is okay, to which he says, "Yes, all is well. I just have a lot of things I need to deal with if we are to be together. I look at him and smile. "So you're house-hunting today, right?" he asks.

"Yes, I am," I reply.

"Good, then please let it be a cosy little cottage with stunning views. Oh, and maybe a pool."

I laugh and say, "You want a pool?"

"Yes, why not?" he says. "We can add a changing block on one end then!" He winks at me, takes a deep breath and leans down to kiss me. "I have to go," he says.

"Okay, so when will I see you?" I ask.

"How about next weekend? I know it's a week away, but I have to get shit sorted." He smiles. "We can order take-out and live like slobs." He laughs when he says it.

"Okay, that sounds amazing," I reply. "I'll unblock your number," I smile.

"Well, I should hope so!" he says in a sexy voice, and I feel nothing but love for this beautiful creature. He kisses me again, then stands to leave, and I feel sad but positive. He gets to the door and turns, blowing me a kiss, which I catch and hold to my heart. Then he opens the door and leaves.

It's not till I'm alone again that I have all the old feelings creep back in. What if he doesn't come back? What if he just said all that to get back in my knickers? I smile and look at my present. But why go to all this effort just to hurt me again? "Okay," I say out loud, "I can't sit and dwell – I have some houses to go see"; and, jumping up, I get dressed and put my hair up in a high ponytail. I'm actually really hungry now, so when I go down for breakfast I order a full English and tuck in.

I arrange to meet Trevor at the first property about two miles away: it's a beautiful cobblestone cottage with really cute windows, and an open fire-place. "Great for winter," says Trevor.

Yeah, and I'm thinking it's great to make love in

front of.

The kitchen is on the small side, but hey, just to look out of the window at the beautiful views of rolling hills would be worth it. I ask Trevor if he has any properties with pools, and his face lights up. "Well, I don't have any with pools, but I do have one that has had plans drawn up to have a pool put in. It's a larger three-bed property, but still gives you that cosy feel."

"Okay, great, let's go see that one," I say.

It's another five miles from Butterwick, in a small village called Freestone, but it's fine. It boasts a popular destination with a more intimate neighbourhood, so I wouldn't feel so isolated.

Come four o'clock, I'm back at the hotel and I'm exhausted. I message Simon and tell him I think I've found the perfect place, to which he replies, 'Fantastic, can't wait to see it.' This makes me smile. I also call the girls and tell them the news; they both seem super-excited for me. I say 'thank you' for telling Simon where I was, and that we have sorted things out. Belle is happy for me, but Jessica is more reserved, saying she meant what she said about hurting him if he leaves me again.

I have some dinner, which is steak and chips, washed down with a lemonade. I've not drunk alcohol for weeks. It's crazy, really: there was a time in my life I couldn't live without it. Nine o'clock comes around and I'm in bed, exhausted from the walking and the emotions of Simon's surprise visit. I send him a text telling him I love him, to which he replies, 'Same'. Okay, so he didn't say it, and he didn't say goodnight; well, maybe he's busy, I tell myself. I soon fall asleep and dream of houses and pools and open fires.

It's Sunday afternoon, and after saying goodbye to Kate and thanking her for a wonderful stay, I'm driving home and the roads are quiet and the sun is bright. I'm listening to Nicky Minaj's 'The Crying Game', and I can't help thinking how empty I was only a few short days ago, and how it can all change in just one night.

Back home, I settle on the sofa with a cup of tea for a quiet night. Simon hasn't phoned me all day or sent me a message. I fiddle with my new bracelet in frustration. I have to be patient; he needs to sort stuff and then he will be in touch. Yes, that's it, just go with it and chill, I tell myself. 'Okay, Ruby,' says my inner bitch, 'you keep telling yourself that.'

As the week goes by, I get more and more concerned. I've not heard from him and I want to message him, but I'm scared in case he doesn't reply. Trevor calls me to say my offer has gone through on the three-bed – and for five thousand less than the asking price. I'm thrilled, because that will help towards the pool. Not that I have to worry about money.

I call the girls and ask them what I should do.

They tell me to wait. It's funny how they went from hating him to actually being on his side. I wait patiently, but by the time Friday comes, I can't stand it any more. Surely he would have been in touch by now if he was planning to come over? So I pluck up the courage to call him. I'm so nervous; what if he's mad at me?

As the phone rings, I contemplate hanging up, but a woman answers on the other end, saying, "Hello, this is Simon's phone." Shit, fuck! "Who's this?" she asks.

"Hello," I say all, confused, "is Simon there, please?"

The woman speaks clearly, "Is that you, Francesca? This is Simon's mother."

What? I'm screaming in my head, who's Francesca? "No," I say with a stutter, "this is Ruby Frankton."

"Oh, sorry, dear, I thought you were Simon's girlfriend."

Wait, what? I hear Simon in the background asking, "Who is it, mum?"

She speaks as if confused, saying, "Someone called Ruby Frankton."

I hear him say, "Fuck!"

I'm seething. Oh, my fucking god! I hang up the phone. I'm shaking uncontrollably – this is too much to deal with. What the hell is going on? She didn't know who I was. He fucking lied to me; he never told her he was going to be with me. Why, though? Why lie to me? Who the fucking hell is Francesca? "Ruby, you are a fucking fool!" I scream into the air.

My phone starts to ring and it's Simon. I press the 'end call' button and throw it on the sofa. I need a fucking drink – for the first time in months I need a goddamned fucking drink. I walk to the kitchen and I'm so thankful I've kept vodka in the fridge for emergencies. My phone rings again, but I don't look. I'm so angry – I'm shaking with anger.

It all makes sense now. Why he's not been in touch – if he truly wanted to be with me, he would be here, he would ring me and message me, like a normal person. I'm a fucking idiot to believe him.

My phone rings again, and again, and again, over and over, but I just let it ring. Thirty minutes later, I hear banging on my door, and it makes me jump. I know it's him, but I don't want to see him. I've downed half the bottle of vodka. He bangs again, calling my name; so, pulling myself up, I walk to the door. He bangs again and again, until I open the door and he barges in, grabbing me and pushing me against the wall. He's mad. "Would it hurt for you to answer your fucking phone, Ruby?" he yells. I'm silent, I can't speak. "Well, fucking answer me."

I look into his eyes and say, "Would it hurt for you to tell me the truth for once in your life?"

He stands back as if I've slapped him. "Ruby, it's not what you think. I'm sorry, but it's not." He's so conflicted, and I can see the pain on his face.

"For what, Simon? What are you sorry for?" He stares at me. "For what, Simon? For fucking lying to me again and again, for making me think yet again you actually fucking wanted me? I'm such a fucking idiot!" I yell, throwing my hands in the air.

"Don't say that," he says, stepping towards me.

I instantly push him back. "Don't you dare come near me!" I snap.

He puts his hands in his pockets. "You're not an idiot, Ruby. I'm the idiot," he says in a defeated voice.

"Yes, Simon, you truly fucking are. You never even told your mother, did you? And who's Francesca? What the fuck, Simon?" He looks at me. "Well?" I scream.

"No, I didn't tell her." He speaks in a low voice, but my eyes are wild. "Francesca is a girl my mother wants me to marry – she is very wealthy and my mother has set me up on a few occasions now to take her out for dinner; I've been keeping her at arm's length to show my mother I'm not interested, but my mother is very persuasive."

I shake my head and the tears flow. "Well, now you don't have to tell her anything, do you? And you can marry whomever your mother desires." I stand with my arms folded and tell him with a heavy heart to please leave.

"Ruby, please don't do this." He comes forward, grabbing me around my waist. I push him back, but he comes at me again. I hit his chest hard, but he kisses me with force and I push him away again.

"No, Simon, you have to fucking leave." I hit him once more. "You will not do this to me ever again."

"Please, Ruby…" He stops and stares at me, but then he grabs me again, kissing me hard. I kiss him back, because I fucking love this man. He is strong, pushing me against the wall, and he yanks down my sweat pants and thong, which fall to the floor and I kick them away. He undoes his jeans and releases the beast, then picks me up with ease and I wrap my legs around him so he can enter my soft, delicate parts. He holds me up against the wall with ease, and I am crying hard, because I know this is the end, I know this has to end. He is moving in and out with a soft, slow rhythm, and I cling to his shoulders, with his head resting in my neck. He is breathing heavy as he spins us around and slowly falls down to his knees, so we are lying on the floor; then he picks up the pace and fucks me with a new need. He is hard and he is fast, and I cry out again and again, and this undoes him – he comes, groaning my name, saying he loves me. I'm crying so much, the sobs are making me shiver, but he holds me for an age, slowly getting up and sitting with his back against the couch. I force myself up and sit on my legs. I can feel the wetness leaking, but I don't care. I need him to leave now.

Finally, he say, "Sorry, I never meant to hurt you again."

"No, Simon," I say, holding up my hands, "I don't want to hear your fucking excuses any more. Please, just fucking leave." I point to the door. I'm a mess; he can see what he's done to me and I know it's killing him, but he had a choice and he chose wrong. I look at him, shaking my head. "I don't ever want to see you again," I add.

"Ruby, no, please," he begs. "I will tell her, I promise. It's just she's a complicated woman."

I stare at his beautiful face for what may be the last time and I say, "No, Simon, she's just being a mother: she wants what's best for you."

"She needs to be told gently," he adds.

"So, Simon," I say, "you're the one who's complicated; and I'm not going to be a part of it any more. I can't; I need to move on, and I need you to leave."

He looks at me for a long time and finally stands and runs his hand through his hair as he moves to the front door. "Ruby, please," he begs, "I need you. Don't do this."

I turn and look at him. "Fucking hurts, doesn't it? Hurts to want someone you can't fucking have." Then I turn away again, and he stands there for a few more seconds and I know he's sniffing back tears, but I don't care. He moves towards me, so I put my hand up as if to stop him, saying, "Please don't." I'm crying so much my eyes hurt.

He stops, stares at me, then turns to leave. I hear

the door click shut and I'm once again alone. The tears flow thicker and faster than ever before and I'm heartbroken once again. I sink to the floor and scream into my lap. It's the hardest thing I've ever done, but I know that this will be the last time – it has to be. I refuse to let him do this to me ever again. I need to move on and find happiness again.

I crawl upstairs and into my bed and I cry myself to sleep. I call the girls the next day and tell them what happened and they come straight over to comfort me. I tell them I just need to move and find a new happiness, and we hug each other for a long time, with Jessica telling me she's going to pull the brake lines on his fancy car.

It's not until I start to pack up my house a few weeks later and put my memories into a box that I start to question my decision. I've blocked Simon's number again, and I've not heard from him at all. Standing here, watching all my things being packed away, makes me sad. I love this house – I always have – but I know it's time to leave. I love everything in this house that reminds me of what I've been through over the years; and, more to the point, this last few months.

Just as the kitchen table is carried out to be placed on the truck, I smile. I have one last wander around my house and I have to stop myself crying: the bathroom, the shower – the door now fixed – my bedroom where my bed once was, now empty, the spare rooms where my girls have stayed on many a drunken night, now empty; then back down to the kitchen, and the living room, also empty, and it's exactly how I feel inside – empty.

I stand and play with the delicate bracelet on my wrist and read the words over and over. I miss him. I blocked him that night, and I made a vow I would never get close to a man like I did him. I'd be lying if I said I didn't think of him, and he will always be close to my heart.

I smile at the girls as they say 'ready?' I take a deep breath and say, "Yes, let's go," so the girls jump in the front of their car and I jump in the back, and we follow the removal van out of my road and I look back at my house and I look back at my for-now car and smile. The girls have offered to drive it back to the rental company for me; as much as I would like to keep it, I know I can't – it wouldn't be fair, plus it's just another reminder of Simon.

We set off for the two-and-a-half-hour drive, and Belle turns on the radio, with Kodaline singing 'All I Want'. I smile and think, 'Yes, at one point you were all I ever wanted, but now you've lost me.' There is only so much a woman can take, and I've taken too much, so we turn it up full blast and sing along.

The roads are empty, the sun is shining, it's a beautiful August day and I'm off to start my new life.